Delectat

Winging

Books in this series so far:

Deliciously Deceased

Delectably Departed

Published in 2018 by Emma L Beal

Copyright © EmmaLBeal2018

Cover Design: Paul Beal MBIE

Emma L Beal has asserted her right to be identified as the author of this work in accordance with the Copyright, Designs and Patents Act 1988.

All rights reserved. No part of this publication may be reproduced, stored in a retrieval system, or transmitted in any form or by any means, electrical, mechanical, photocopying, recording or otherwise without the prior permission of the copyright owner.

All characters appearing in this work are fictitious. Any resemblance to real persons, living or dead is purely coincidental.

Chapter One

I would like to say that I am excited at the prospect of working undercover within a beauty spa, however based on the facts and information that I have; I truly do not believe that any beauty treatment is worth dying for!

So here are the facts as I know them:

The company that I am going undercover for is called 'Pearl Beauty Spa and Detox Centre.' Check out their luscious business card:-

The company are using products that will either:

- Scar you for life.
- Kill you.

Not exactly a great advertisement is it!

The managing director has gone into hiding and nobody has a clue where she is.

Celestia has made this a major priority as her best friend (also deceased) has a daughter who is booked in for treatment in one week's time. Yikes!

Keeping up?
Good, because it gets better...I have full, signed, sealed and delivered 100% authorisation to be myself! And as you all know this is a pretty big deal for me!

- The plan of action?

Oh come on! As if you honestly believed that I would have a plan! Hardly!

I should really explain my situation to avoid any confusion that could potentially arise, for those of you not already clued up.
I am dead.

I was murdered and my poor little body was left abandoned outside of Oxfam, I mean seriously! Oxfam!
My beautiful face was slashed, and I had been stabbed viciously through the heart in what can only be described as a frenzied attack. Thankfully I have not yet recovered all of my memories from that evening, and I truly hope that I never do.

After I was murdered I arrived in Heaven in the longest queue ever known to man in the hope that I would contemplate my life in a nice serene manner; however I had an argument with a chav, Tracey, who I am now very good friends with and was pulled from the queue. I humiliated myself by picking on a grieving mother, Victoria, another person that I am now friends with, in fact I actually played a major part in reuniting her with her deceased daughter which she was eternally grateful for. I have to say it was a really beautiful moment seeing her reunited with her little girl Sophie.

I learnt that the girl I had thought of as my best friend, Juliana, was in fact anything but and that she was solely responsible for the death of her little sister Maisie, who I have since met in Heaven. She seems to be doing well.

Children have their own sector in Heaven so that they do not have to mingle with the adult's full time, which makes sense. I mean there are so many suicides and victims of murder up here, the children really do not need to be surrounded by such agony. There is a shared garden which is stunning and incredibly peaceful, the sun always shines and it is the perfect location for children to play and sadly see their parents or other adult family members that may have passed away.

Juliana joined the queue when she too was murdered, unfortunately for her she was sent directly to Hell because of what she did to Maisie. Justly deserved if I am honest.

Seeing her go however was horrendous and I fear I will forever see the way she burned from the inside out. I still do not understand why she did it and I do not suppose that I ever will.

I met Celestia, the Queen Bee of Heaven. She hated me on

sight and the feeling quite frankly was mutual. After giving me a serious make under, she sent me back down to earth to solve my murder, accompanied by Daniel Fox, my guardian and the new love of my life, or rather death. Daniel was murdered in a case of mistaken identity, he was shot in the face when he was leaving work one evening, he seems okay about it now, which gives me hope that eventually I will be okay about my death.

I met a creepy embalmer called Damien though in the end he turned out to be fairly normal and I guess I could say rather nice. I cannot lie though, he is dreadfully dull.

I made friends with a group of girls that I would never have normally entertained in life and had my face smashed in on a piñata donkey, well, a photograph of my face anyway.

What a pleasant evening that was... not!

My so called friends were pleased that I was dead, however their joy was short lived as most of them were also killed. I did try to stop it happening, truly I did, but I just could not figure out who the killer was fast enough to prevent it.

We did eventually crack the case and a girl called Gemma was arrested, basically she was enraged over being shunned as a child by our friend Monica, seems pretty lame a reason if you ask me. Gemma came from the lower classes and truth be told we had no idea that Monica had once come from a working class background, she seemed to fit the socialite role perfectly. Gemma hated what Monica had become and in turn hated everything about all of us. We were even given the nickname 'Superiors' because we believed ourselves to be Superior to everybody else, they were not wrong.

In life I was a rich bitch bully, I cared for no one but myself and my wealth which in the end became my demise. I have learnt a lot of tough lessons since arriving in Heaven and whilst I feel that I have changed immeasurably, I know that I will always have a smart mouth and a sassy attitude, that is just me and despite trying my hardest to change, some things are just ingrained indefinitely.

I feel that I can make some amends however for my previous behaviour by cracking this case for Celestia; I am not going to fail this time.

Celestia has me set up in a little apartment right next door to her friend's daughter Jodie Winters, this way I can at least be close enough to her to make sure that she does not go through with the treatment at Pearl, and I have to admit that my apartment is beautiful despite being a tad on the small size.

I requested two bedrooms, Celestia as you can imagine protested to the high heavens about that as she does with pretty much everything regarding me, but when I explained that a second bedroom would be required in case I needed Tracey's help with the situation, she soon came around to my way of thinking.

My apartment is on the top floor and has a balcony which overlooks the City Centre, it has two bedrooms both of which are en-suite, and they are decorated neutrally which is nice and tasteful. The lounge and kitchen are both open plan which I did not think I would like at first, but as the apartment is a little on the small side it surprisingly opens it up quite well.

It is only a ten minute walk away from Pearl Beauty Spa which is also a bonus as public transport is just not an option for me. Can you honestly imagine me surrounded by all of those people? Perspiring, dirty, noisy plebs. No Thank you!

I know, I know, it doesn't exactly sound like I have changed, but I am right, vagrants do use buses as well!

In order for me to keep up the pretence of being alive, living in Leeds and being a normal everyday person who has rent and bills to pay, not to mention fooling Jodie, I have to do the unthinkable... I must go to work.

Celestia has somehow managed to get me a receptionist position working within Pearl Beauty Spa. The owner Alicia King has gone into hiding but from what I can gather she still wants to keep the spa open for as long as she can, and for that she requires staff. There is one other girl that works there and I feel that she must be the one dishing out the deadly treatments.

I have never worked a day in my life so god only knows how this is going to pan out, then again how hard can it be answering a telephone?

I start my new job in one week's time, which gives me plenty of extra time to befriend Jodie and try to talk her out of this lunacy. I just hope that I can get her to see sense and drop it. I haven't yet figured out how to get near to her without coming across as a total loser stalker, but I will figure it out.

I have tried to contact Daniel to ask for his advice but he is also working undercover. He did not go into too much detail about his case; he just briefly told me that it involves gangs and drugs. If he were not already dead I would be seriously worried about him. I am sure that he will respond to me when it is safe to do so.

I do miss him terribly though, it feels like we were just

getting somewhere and then we were called away to different cases, I hope that we can both clear them quickly and have some time for us. I appreciate that we have nothing but time now, but I still think that we need to be alone for a while to see where this relationship is going. I love him that much I do know.

I guess only time will tell.

Chapter Two

It turns out that the walls are paper thin in my new apartment, which means that not only have I discovered that the occupants of the flat to my right are swingers, but also that Jodie who lives to my left has some serious boyfriend issues.

From what I have overheard her boyfriend is ridiculously insecure and demanding, I deduce this by the amount of time she spends on the telephone comforting him and reassuring him that yes he is the only one for her, and that no of course she won't be going out without him again, and yes of course she really misses him. Barf! When I finally meet her I am going to put this straight. Dominating, over bearing so called boyfriends are just not the way forward. The swingers are a completely different kettle of fish however. I now know that a Candie and a Roberto live to the right of me, and that Candie likes it when Patrick comes over with his feather duster (I do not even want to imagine what that is about) and Roberto likes it when Helena comes over in her red stockings, but that Candie hates Helena and Roberto hates Patrick, (the arguments are legendary). Go figure.

And I thought being dead was complicated.

Since moving here I have come across quite a mix of people, usually in the lift, which is often a disturbing situation to find yourself in. I am at least ninety percent sure that the couple who live on the bottom floor in apartment number three are zombies as they only ever come out at night and always seem a little dopey and sluggish. I have also met the woman who lives on the second floor, apartment number fourteen, she is slightly bizarre in that she never speaks, she just stares, which can I just say is freaky when you are stuck in a lift with her. There are also two lawyers, a nurse, a lap dancer and a builder, see, quite a mix.

My life has changed so much since dying. I know for a fact that I would never had mixed with these kinds of people when I was still alive, I would most definitely have gone out of my way to avoid them. But now I find that I enjoy the variety, I look forward to it even. All I have to do now is rein in my old self and get Jodie to let me in.

I was going to use the 'could I please borrow some sugar' routine that I always see in films to get my friendship with Jodie started, but I figured that was too lame so I am going instead with a rather boring but effective knock on the door to introduce myself with. Here's hoping that she is warm and welcoming and not a cold fish, because I seriously have no backup plan whatsoever for being rejected. I suppose should all else fail then I could check in with Jodie's mother as she is also dead and the reason that I am here.

Celestia has made it perfectly clear to me that I cannot fail on this and that she will give me as many resources as she can to stop the potential death of Jodie and countless many others who may choose to use this beauty spa, I just hope that I do not let her down.

It turns out that Celestia and Jodie's mother Eileen go way back, which fully explains why she is so edgy about this case. They were practically like sisters when they were younger and Eileen was devastated when Celestia died, but now that they are both deceased they get to see each other all of the time, which is lovely and sad at the same time I suppose. Nobody at all was devastated when I died, losers!

Knocking on Jodie's door I wait impatiently for her to answer. I know that she is in there because I have heard her pottering about and hoovering. I am just about to knock again when the door is slowly eased open and I am faced with one tear filled eye staring out at me.

'Yes?' she asks me timidly. 'Can I help you?'

'I just wished to introduce myself, I'm Tiffany, I have just moved in next door to you.'

'Oh, okay.' she mutters.

'Are you okay?' I ask, 'It's just you seem a little upset.'

'I'm fine, really. Well, if that's all I best get back in.'

'You don't look fine.' I continue, 'in fact you...'

'Well I am!' she snaps at me furiously, 'what the hell do you want?!'

As she prepares to slam the door into my concerned face I see the black eye that she was evidently trying to hide.

'Well if you are okay then how did you get that?' I question.

'Why are you so bloody nosy? I don't even know you! If you must know I fell over the rug and bashed my face on the corner of the coffee table, satisfied?'

Peering over her shoulder I shake my head in ever growing concern, 'I suppose I would have been if you actually had a rug.'

'What?' looking around her she sees what I have seen, a big fat rugless nothing. 'I...well I got rid of it after the accident, it's obviously a death trap. What has it got to do with you anyway?'

'Look I know that we have just met, but if you need any

help, or you just want to talk about things then I am here, okay? Literally one door away.' I smile at her warmly in the hope that it might thaw her iciness towards me, she does not smile back.

'Just go away.' she sobs and slams the door in my face. Great! Now what?!

As I am turning to leave and pondering what the hell I am going to do next, I hear the door open behind me and a little voice asking me if I would like to come in for a cup of tea. I accept and find myself sitting in Jodie's flat trying to coax information from her about this mysterious black eye, though to be honest I already have my suspicions.

'My friends said that Dwight isn't any good for me, but what can I do? I know that he loves me, and really I know that I shouldn't have wound him up about the stripper at Claire's hen party, but it was just so funny and I really wanted to share my fun with him. I shouldn't have made him angry, I know that I shouldn't. They said I should just drop him.' She is wringing her hands and I can see the stress and anxiety scrunching up her otherwise beautiful face. 'I know that he loves me really, and he was super sorry afterwards, that has to mean something, right? I'm gonna get this facial done at a place called Pearl and I'm really hoping that it will help me get rid of these.' She points angrily towards the dark circles and the bruising under her eyes and begins to sob again. 'Dwight wants me to go; What do you think?'

At last, an opening. Best to tread carefully though I think. 'Look Jodie I don't want to be the bearer of bad news honey but this Dwight character is not treating you like he loves you, I mean look at your face, he did that to you. Your friends were right, you do need to kick him to the curb, you deserve better than him. You must know deep down that you do. How long has this been going on for?'

'Only the one time...he loves me, and he said sorry.' she cries.

'He's a liar Jodie and he will absolutely do it again, that I can promise you!'

'You don't even know him!'

'No thank god! Will you at least take some time off from him and evaluate your situation? Please?'

She looks uncertain, 'but I have my facial and he will want to see me after that.'

'Why are you doing this to please him? And have you not heard what is going on at the moment at Pearl? People are dying for crying out loud! Do you really want to put your life at risk for this bloody Dwight?'

'If it were so bad then they wouldn't still be open would they!' she snaps.

'They are only open because they haven't been found guilty of anything yet, at the moment it is all rumour and speculation.'

'Exactly!'

'No not exactly.' I argue back, 'If there was nothing to be concerned about then why has the owner vanished into thin air? Why have all of these people put in so many complaints to the company and to the police? Think about it Jodie it just doesn't add up.'

'Well I am going and nothing that you say will change my mind.' she sulks.

'Great! Can you at least take some time out from Dwight then? For me?'

'I don't even know you, why would I listen to you? I'm sorry that I told you, it was stupid of me.'

'Yes well, sometimes strangers are the best people to talk to and hand out advice.'

'Whatever. I'll think about it alright. I have to get ready now, I'm meeting an old acquaintance for dinner, and god only knows what she is going to make of this.' she points worriedly to her black eye and the tears begin again.

Smiling I grab her hand and drag her towards my apartment. 'Now that I can absolutely help with, you just leave your pretty face to me. I have more cosmetics than Clarins.' She laughs nervously, but I know that I have just sealed our friendship, hopefully in time to save her life.

'Are you seeing anybody special?' Jodie asks me whilst I add the finishing touches to her now none visible black eye.

'I sure am.' I smile, 'his name is Daniel. He is working away at the moment though.'

'That's a shame, we could have double dated.' she giggles nervously.

'I thought we had agreed you were going to take some time away from him?'

'No, you decided that, I haven't decided anything yet. Anyway enough of that, let me see myself.' Grabbing the mirror she gasps at her now perfectly smooth face and says over and over that she can't believe it is her. 'Oh thank you so much, I look amazing!' she laughs. 'Marsha will never know that I have a right shiner hiding under this lot.'

Taking the mirror from her I shake my head as I start to put away my make-up, 'you shouldn't even have had to worry about that, because it should never have been there and you know it.'

'He didn't mean it Tiffany, he really didn't.'

'Know that for a fact do you?' I demand.

'How can I know for sure if I don't see him again?' she questions me, 'if I follow your instructions to never see him again then how will I ever know?'

'And what if the next time you see him he decides to beat you black and blue and put you in a hospital? For crying out loud Jodie he is a waste of space oxygen thief and you need to stay far far away from him.'

'I can't' she yells, 'I love him!'

'Please I am begging you, stay away from him.'

Standing up she flattens down her skirt, takes a deep breath and turns to leave, 'thank you for everything today.' she whispers, 'it means a lot to me.'

'Anytime.' I reply, but I am talking to the closed door.

I just do not know what to do with Jodie, I know that she understands that what Dwight did was wrong and that she should never go back to him, but it is like she is stuck in this fantasy land where she thinks that he will change, and that if he says sorry enough times then eventually he really will be. I wish I could make her understand that he has struck her once and it will not be the last time. Men like him do not change, fact!

Picking up the phone I dial the numbers and prepare to leave this mortal coil once more. (We have gone all modern now; phone boxes have now been replaced with mobile phones in order for us to get back to Heaven, thank god, literally). I need to speak with Tracey, see if she has any ideas on what I can do now.

I need help, because if it isn't the beauty spa that kills Jodie then I have no doubts that Dwight eventually will.

I wonder if Tracey is free for a little investigative work. I feel a honey trap heading Dwight's way.

Chapter Three

Heaven is bursting at the seams as usual with possible new additions and I have to admit that I find it bizarrely comforting. The queue is once more riddled with undesirables which quite frankly makes my skin crawl, but I am confident that they will not be hanging around making the place look untidy for much longer. Heaven only takes the best and I am proof of that, obviously.

'Tiff, Tiff! Over here mate!' Tracey is yelling at me whilst walking from the restaurant and I feel instantly overwhelmed to see her. What has happened to me up here? 'Quick before she sees you.' she laughs.

'Before who sees me?' I enquire suspiciously, laughing at her odd behaviour.

'The Matron of course. Jeez Tiff you have been gone what? A week?'

'Matron? Tracey I really must insist that you explain yourself.'

'Her, see?' she points towards a rather large woman slowly plodding down the corridor with a very stern look upon her weathered face. 'The Matron.' she declares. 'She's a right battleaxe, seriously Tiff I do not wanna get on the wrong side of her. She had poor Jennifer in tears yesterday, just because she dared to loiter in the corridor for a few seconds.'

'Oh my god Tracey, how can she possibly be that stern, she looks like a downtrodden Miss Trunchbull!' We both erupt into hysterics, tears rolling down our cheeks as we lean against each other, weak with laughter.

'Ladies, please be quiet!' The Matron's voice booms down the corridor making Tracey jump. 'People are trying to reflect here, in peace and serenity; they do not need to be disrupted by your childish behaviour. Move along.'

'Reflecting?' I sneer, 'I think you will find that it is called contemplating, as in they are contemplating their life, do you need me to explain?'

'I do not need you to explain, I do however need you to move away from the corridor and let these people continue with their reflecting in peace.'

'What exactly are you doing here anyway?' I ask, curiously. 'What is your purpose?'

'C'mon Tiff.' urges Tracey whilst yanking on my arm, 'we should just go.'

'No, I truly do want to know, what exactly she is the Matron of?'

'I am the Matron of the corridor, I am here to...'

'So has the corridor done anything suspicious lately? Should we be on high alert? Total lockdown?' I snigger.

'You are deliberately mocking me.' she snaps, 'I am here to patrol the corridor and ensure that all arrivals are able to reflect peacefully with minimal disruptions.'

'Okaaaay! Well that sounds horrendously dull. Come on Tracey; let's leave Matron here with her corridor.'

'If I see you hanging around here again I will have no choice but to report you to Celestia and also the law services. Good day girls.'

'Sorry, come again? The law services?' I ask curiously.

'Yes.' she responds authoritatively, 'I will have you dragged up in front of the judges before you can even utter the word contemplating, understood?'

'You crack me up Matron; I mean seriously, you really do

crack me up.'

'I suggest that you ask Celestia about Heavenly Law and see what she says, clearly you are ignorant in these matters.'

'Ignorant? Why you...'

'C'mon Tiff, we should bail.' Tracey grabs my arm and drags me away from the Matron. Rest assured however that this is not over; nobody calls me ignorant, nobody!

Banging on Celestia's door, despite Tracey's protestations I wait angrily for her to answer. Who the hell does she think she is anyway? threatening me... the cheek of it!

The door swings open and Celestia looks surprised to see me, 'Tiffany? Case closed already?'

'What? No, I just came to get Tracey. Look Celestia we just had a run in with the crazy corridor keeper down there and she threatened me with judges, I mean what the hell?'

'By crazy corridor keeper am I to take it you mean Myra'

'Oh Myra, figures.' I instantly think of the nutso moors murderer Myra Hindley and inwardly cringe. Myra indeed. 'What is her deal?'

'Her deal? If you mean what is she doing then I shall explain. Myra is the new Matron of the corridor, you have to admit that it is quite easy to disrupt contemplation; you have done this on more than one occasion yourself Tiffany. Myra's presence on the corridor will put an end to that, which can only be a good thing. After all, we do not want people to lose their train of thought and end up in Heaven when we know that they belong elsewhere, do we?'

'I suppose not.' I agree reluctantly. 'But how do you stop the people in the queue from seeing the people in front burning? Is she going to prevent that also?'

'No of course she isn't, don't be silly Tiffany. We have changed things a little whilst you have been away. Now when contemplation ends for a person heading elsewhere a curtain will automatically go around them, preventing everybody else from seeing them leave.'

'Oh. Well I suppose that makes sense. But what about when she isn't there? What if somebody dares to go into the corridor in her absence?'

'Myra never leaves the corridor; she has rooms just off of it. She is really very well set up there, no need to mingle, which is just the way that she likes it.'

'Oh my god, what a loser!' I mutter under my breath. 'Well she threatened me with Heavenly Law Celestia and I am not pleased, I didn't even do anything wrong.'

'Now that I find hard to believe.' she laughs, 'Tiffany Delamarre innocent? Mmmm, debatable.'

'I am serious! Tracey and I were just catching up and she went all schizo on us and threatened to drag us before the judges. Is this a new addition also?'

'No Tiffany, Heavenly Law has always been around. She was just trying to worry you, trust me if you were ever placed before the judges you would have had to have done something extremely bad, and as terrible as you can be I do not think hanging around the corridor constitutes a trip to the cells, so relax.'

'Cells?' squeaks Tracey, 'we have cells?'

'Indeed we do, however I sincerely doubt that either of you ladies will ever see them, so please, stop panicking. Now Tiffany, how are things going with Jodie? Have you made any real progress as of yet? Has she cancelled the appointment?'

'Oh Celestia, I fear that the appointment is not the only thing that her mother should be concerned about. Did you know that this boyfriend of hers, Dwight, beats her? I am worried for her safety.'

'I did not know that. Are you absolutely sure?'

'Beyond sure! You should have seen the size of the black eye that he gave her, she's a mess.'

'And her appointment? when is that?'

'The day after I start working there, so I am hoping that I can take that opportunity to maybe cancel the appointment on the computer and bide myself some time. I think she is having the treatment because Dwight wants her to and she is too scared to say no.'

'And where does Tracey fit into this?'

'Well...' I grin at Tracey, 'I was hoping to use Tracey as a honey trap, get him hooked and then scare the living daylights out of him so that he stays well clear of Jodie.'

Tracey squeals in delight and I have to laugh, it isn't often that she gets to leave Heaven, so this will be a rare treat for her.

'And Tracey will be staying in the apartment with you?'

'She certainly will. I think if we can get Jodie away from Dwight then she will change her mind about the treatment.'

'Okay Tiffany, do what you must to put an end to this. Do you think that whilst you are undercover you may be able to find the location of the missing owner? If that were possible then you could question her and gather the proof needed to ensure that the entire operation is shut down.'

'I will certainly try my best. Are the lab guys still running checks on what is in the products?'

'Yes, you must bear with them though; their inexperience

is slowing them down a touch. In their defence they weren't exactly qualified when they died.'

The lab guys here in Heaven were killed when a stupid student prank in the laboratory went wrong; needless to say they did not complete their studies.

'Of course. I take it the police are not running checks or anything?'

'At the moment no, they only have complaints from the public at the moment and they seem to not be taking them seriously.'

'But people have died!' fumes Tracey. 'People have been left scarred for life!'

'Yes they have, but the police force are stretched and without concrete proof they won't waste valuable resources on rumours and complaints.'

'I will do my best to find her.' I confirm, 'And Tracey and I will put a stop to this Dwight character, won't we Tracey?' 'Hells yeah we will! He's finished!'

'I'm looking forward to being roomies for a bit Tiff. I never had a roomie before. To be fair I never had a friend to be a roomie with before.'

'Well guess what Tracey? You have me now, and I cannot wait. We are going to have such a blast, and that fool Dwight is not going to know what has hit him.'

'Amen to that.' shouts Tracey, 'Amen to that!'

Chapter Four

'...now just press the tab key, then the little save button down there and you are done.' Clapping her hands in delight Kimberley double checks my work and then takes a big gulp of her Costa coffee, 'See I knew you would get the hang of it straight away, easy peasy.'

Never have I wanted to slap a face so much in my life.

Kimberley Payne (the name fits) is the only remaining member of staff at Pearl and she is driving me nuts. She has long red hair, even longer legs and is falling out of her teeny size six dress. She is beautiful, in need a good meal and a personality transplant, but beautiful. So far this morning I have been shown how to use the kettle, I mean seriously! How to answer the telephone and now how to use the computer to book appointments. Now, I appreciate that I have never worked a day in my life and had I been left to work out the computerised system by myself then I would have no doubt killed it, but the telephone?

The interior of the beauty spa is how I imagined it would be, to be honest they all look the same. All white furniture, glass tables, soft music playing, expensive looking artwork and doors cryptically marked private. I wonder if they are where Kimberley works on the clients. Well there is only way to way to find out.

'What is behind that door?' I ask sweetly, pointing to it.

'That one?' she replies dumbly.

Duh! 'Yes, that one.' Is this girl for real?

'Oh that's just a treatment room, you know, for like facials.'

'Are you really still doing those? Hasn't the negative publicity put people off?'

She laughs, 'Absolutely not, if anything it has drawn them in. You see Tiffany, the way these girls look at it is simple, if people are talking about it then it must be good. Even negative comments can be good for business.'

'Then you have me confused.' I begin, 'If business is going well then why has the owner vanished off of the face of the earth? You think she would be lapping this up.'

'She hasn't vanished, she's just taking a well earned sabbatical from the beauty world.'

'Sure.' I murmur.

'No really she is. Alicia has worked tirelessly to promote her business, her baby. Can you imagine what it must have been like to receive those dreadful hate letters, she was gutted. So yeah, she's having a well deserved break.'

'And leaving you here all alone to man the shop?'

'But I'm not alone, you're here now.' she smiles. 'Pass me that magazine there will you.' she points towards a glass table tucked away in the corner, 'it is so out of date, can't be having the clients thinking we are so behind the times.'

Reaching over to retrieve the offending glossy magazine I pass it across to her and pray for the four millionth time that this day will end.

'Oh my god.' she shrieks, 'I forgot all about this. Oh how could I.'

'Erm....are you okay?' I ask, not really that interested in her answer.

'Look, just look.' She thrusts the magazine my way and slowly sits down, 'oh it's all just too emotional.'

'Flicking open the front cover in feigned interest I almost shriek myself when I see the face smiling up at me! You have got to be kidding. 'Oh my god!'

'I know right? She was just so beautiful, a true ambassador of the company and now we will never ever see her again thanks to that evil cow Tiffany!'

Staring up at me from the second page is none other than my murderess ex best friend Juliana Victor! What on earth was she doing modelling for this lot and why the hell didn't I know? And... 'excuse me?' I demand, 'How was Juliana's death the fault of Tiffany Delamarre?

'Because if she hadn't have gotten mixed up with her then she would still be alive. You look a bit like her you know, Tiffany I mean, well obviously I don't mean Juliana.' She laughs again and I want to scream. 'Do you get that a lot? the similarities? especially with you having the same name and everything.'

'Not really no.' I lie.

'Well that surprises me a little, but I suppose your eyes are why nobody asks.' She busies herself reading the article that I am sure she has read a million times, and I reign in the urge to give her a different coloured eye of her very own.

'So what did Juliana do here?' I ask, interrupting her reading and receiving a tut for my question.

'Wow, where have you been hiding? She was the face of Pearl. Why do you think people are begging for appointments? It's because they want to look like her. Oh my god she was practically best mates with Alicia, they did everything together. And then she was killed. So can you now understand why Alicia needs this time away? She's not only exhausted but she's in mourning as well.'

I lie and say that yes I can now understand and that I am going to just nip outside for some fresh air, she doesn't even look up from her magazine. Rude!

Juliana was the face of Pearl! Oh my actual days. She was practically best friends with the owner? This is pure gold, or at least it would be if she wasn't in Hell. Dammit Juliana. Why did you have to go and be a murdering loser!

After successfully cancelling Jodie's appointment and rescheduling her in for another consultation in six days time (it was the best I could do) I make my way back to Heaven, bypass Myra the Maniac and head directly for Tracey's room.

Tracey is busy packing her things so that she can move in with me for a little while and as I begin to remove items from her suitcase to fold them properly she laughs at me and calls me a control freak.

'Believe me when you unpack at my place you will be grateful for this.'

'Yeah yeah.' she laughs. 'So anymore news on Jodie?'

I fill her in on managing to cancel her appointment at Pearl and all about Juliana's weird appearance there.

'Christ Tiff, that's such a bummer, there's no way of speaking to her now.'

'Well...' I begin, 'there might actually be one way that I can do this.'

'Hate to disappoint you beautiful but she's in Hell, rightfully so, and you are in Heaven, there is no way around it.'

'I believe that there is, but I am going to need your help.'

The corridor is quiet, too quiet. Myra must be lurking around somewhere, ready to pounce.

'Just run the plan past me again.' Tracey whispers, 'I wanna be sure I've got it right.'

'Okay, so if you distract Myra I can sneak past her, pick somebody that is on the verge of departing the queue and hitch a ride.'

'Okaaay, and how are you going to know who is about to depart?'

'That I will just have to figure out when I get there, surely somebody is heading downstairs. Luckily for me the curtains have been introduced so I will be hidden'

'Erm...Tiff, what if you burn as well?'

I hadn't thought of that to be honest, but I need to do this.

'I guess I will find out soon enough won't I.'

'Maybe I should come with you mate, just in case things don't pan out.'

'I can't risk two of us Tracey, not to mention I am going to be seriously reprimanded for this if I am caught, Heavenly Law could be on my horizon.'

'Mates stick together.' she grins, 'C'mon it'll be a blast.'

'I can't Tracey, just cover for me okay?'

Peeking around the corner she declares that the corridor is clear and I should make a run for it now, here's hoping that I can find a bad person and sharpish.

I begin my sprint, thankful that I chose flat shoes for this escapade. Behind me I hear Tracey cry out and turn to see her laying on the floor pretending to have a sprained ankle with Myra looking over her suspiciously, thank god for Tracey. I am halfway down the queue and have not managed to locate a ride to Hell, what am I going to do?

Tracey's moans of pain are echoing down the corridor and I can't help but snigger, Myra is going to kill us for this if she finds out that we tricked her.

To my left a mechanical whirring begins to sound and I know that it is now or never. The curtain is drawing around the soon to be new occupant of Hell. Taking one last look down the corridor I sneak behind the curtain and grab hold of my taxi.

This is it. Please do not let me burn, please!

I am surprised to feel nothing as the man that I am clutching onto burns right in front of my eyes; I had expected a little warmth, minimum, but nothing.

As the floor beneath our feet opens up I suppress my scream of horror and hold onto the man even tighter. We are lowered slowly at first, the darkness creeping up over us like fog, why is this moron not even reacting? Is he completely comatose? Picking up speed now we descend quickly into the deep dark depths of the unknown, and I have never been so scared in my whole life. Hell here I come.

Chapter Five

Hell is blue, the colour not the feeling. Security is a little light and they do not have a Matron or a corridor, or a queue. People are milling about laughing and joking and I can only assume that they are workers not inmates. Surely the Devil would not just let psychopaths wonder around at their own leisure? Could Hell really be this lax?

I have no idea where to start looking for Juliana; do they have a sector for killers of children?

'May I help you?' The voice is deep and sexy, 'Tiffany.'

Turning to face the ridiculously gorgeous man I ask him how he knows my name.

Laughing he takes my hand, 'I know everything, after all this is my home.'

The Devil! The Devil is right in front of me and I am pained to say it but he is beautiful! Shaking my head out of the weird trance that was taking over my frazzled brain I tell him that I am looking for somebody and could he please point me in the right direction.

'Take tea with me Tiffany and I will help you as best as I am able. This way.'

He leads me to a rather charming room, all chrome and black, but not in a gothic creepy way. In fact it is beautifully decorated.

'So, where are all of the flames and torture chambers? I have to admit to feeling a little let down by Hell so far.'

'Answer me this, why would you believe that Hell would be a place of suffering and degradation? I am a bad person am I not? Why would you assume then that I would make other likeminded people suffer?'

'So you mean to tell me that Hell is one big eternal party for lunatics? Are you all living the high life down here then? Sounds nuts.'

'You believe what the book incorrectly tells you, it is one of life's biggest misconceptions you know. There is no burning in Hell.'

'If by the book you mean the Holy Bible then yes I suppose all of my information has come from there.' I shake my head in disbelief at the situation, 'how could they all have it so wrong?'

'Have you ever met a person that has been to Hell and returned to tell the story? No I didn't think so. Yet so many people on the verge of death declare that they have seen the light, they return full of hope that death will be the beginning of something wonderful. If only they knew how brutal that decision process will be, if only they knew that the light they see is just a glimmer of that ridiculous and rather pathetic corridor. Your so called Holy Bible preaches of forgiveness and turning the other cheek, and yet was I forgiven? No, I was banished from the pearly gates and had to forge my own existence, naturally I would surround myself with likeminded people.'

'You tried to usurp God from his throne; I mean seriously, did you think that would have a good outcome?'

'But I ask you again, where was my forgiveness? He will have you make peace with killers and rapists, and yet I was thrown out because I wanted a little promotion, C'mon surely you can see the double standards here?'

'You tried to stab God in the back and steal his job, that is beyond underhanded, no wonder he kicked you out. What about child killers, paedophiles, surely you do not mingle with those monsters?'

'Of course not, what kind of a freak do you think I am? Monstrosities such as those have a special little area, would you like to see?'

'Are they being tortured for all eternity?' Is Juliana in there I wonder.

'Would it please you if I said yes?'

'It would please me if you told me the truth.'

'I can absolutely assure you that they are living out the rest of eternity in darkness and despair. They will never know a moment's peace; they will never feel safe or carefree. Their very existence now is filled with terror and dread, you see Tiffany, I may be evil incarnate but I do have my limits.'

'Why are you here?' I ask boldly, 'you could have had a great time in Heaven with nice people, decent people, and yet you choose to surround yourself with evil, it makes no sense. Why do you prefer these people to the ones in Heaven? Why do you make people do bad things?'

'So many questions Tiffany.' he laughs, 'let me however put one thing immediately to rest. I do not and never have had any influence on what people may or may not do, they walk their own paths, in the end that path may lead them to Heaven's door, or it may lead them to mine.'

'I am sorry but I just do not believe that! If that were true then how can you explain children that kill?'

'You think that I turn innocent children into murderers?' He laughs and despite the fact that he is the Devil it is the sexiest laugh I have ever heard. 'Tiffany Delamarre some children are just born 'not right' they have bad in them, others I blame their upbringing for, whatever the reason you can rest assured it has nothing to do with me. Do you think that every nice person, every generous charitable person is that way because God nipped down to earth one day and made it so? No, they are that way because they were born that way, pure and simple.'

I cannot believe that I am having a debate on killers and the Holy Bible with Satan, he has thrown a few things in there however that have got me thinking.

'So what do you do down here with the people that you don't have in segregation?'

'We party of course!'

'Oh give me a break! You are partying with the likes of Harold Shipman, Hitler and Jack the Ripper? Seriously?'

'Of course. Tiffany these are my people.'

'How can you even like them? I mean Hitler for crying out loud! Are you telling me that you condone what he did?'

'Of course not, but he can no longer continue with his previous ways now that he is here, so I say live and let live. He's actually quite an intelligent man.'

'He is a mass murderer! You need help. I'm thinking along the lines of the straight jacket, padded room variety.'

'I am the Devil sweetheart, what did you honestly expect?'

'I would like to see Juliana Victor now. Please.'

'As you wish, though I would just like to remind you of our earlier conversation in relation to killers of children.'

He smirks and I want to slap his stupid handsome face.

'Are you trying to tell me that she is being tortured? Is she in segregation?'

'Of course, where else would she be? Did you think she would get off lightly because she is a woman?'

'No, of course not, but....'

'It can't be one rule for her and another for everyone else, she killed a child and therefore she is where all child killers go. End of.'

'Okay, then I suggest you show me where she is so that I can get this done and get out of here.'

'Follow me.'

The cells are tiny and dark, so incredibly dark. All around me screams of pain and terror echo. I put my hands over my ears and yet the noise still makes its way through, I do not know what is happening to these people, and to be perfectly honest I do not want to know.

The smell is horrendous, stale urine, sweat and faeces. The Devil was not embellishing the truth when he said that they would suffer.

Juliana's cell is cramped and through the rusty bars I can see her tiny frame, dishevelled, ruined. I know that she killed Maisie, and I am trying my hardest to keep that to the forefront of my mind but the screams are driving me insane. How is a person supposed to have a coherent thought in this dump?

'You have five minutes.'

Walking closer to the cell I softly whisper her name, she does not hear me, but then who could above this noise.

'JULIANA!' I yell, 'JULIANA IT IS ME TIFFANY.' Her tiny body begins to stir and as she turns to face me I let out a scream of my own. Her long blonde hair is so unkempt and there are large clumps missing from it. Looking past her into the cell I see the missing clumps and realise with a start that she has done this to herself, no doubt driven to insanity by being in this place.

'Juliana, please I need to speak with you.' I lean in closer to the bars and pray that she isn't too far gone. Do prayers even work down here?

'Go away Tiffany!' she spits, 'look what you have done to

me!'

'Oh hardly! You did this to yourself when you pushed your little sister off of a cliff.'

The groaning and screaming is becoming frenzied, the prisoners are rattling their cages and trying to reach through the bars to touch me. 'Juliana I need your help, please.' I beg. 'Maybe you can redeem yourself by helping me.' I suggest.

She looks up at me with tear stained eyes, 'you can get me out of here?' she whimpers.

'I'm sorry but...'

'THEN GO TO HELL YOURSELF!' She screams at me with pure hatred. I run from the stinky cells, desperate to be away from this place, from these demented losers.

Running as fast as my legs will carry me I bump straight into the Devil himself.

'Get out of my way.' I demand, pushing him away from me.

'Just one last question Tiffany Delamarre.' He smirks, 'Just how were you planning on leaving exactly?'

Great! I am stuck!

'I'll tell you what, I will personally escort you back to Heaven if you do something for me.'

'I am not doing anything for you.' I reply acidly, 'do I look like I want to end up in one of those disgusting little cells? No way!'

Laughing he steers me towards a door that was most definitely not there a few moments ago. 'Now did I say anything about wanting you to do something bad?'

'Well....no.'

'Read the book again for me.'

'That is it? Read the Holy Bible and you will let me

leave?'

'Yes. Now that you have met me and seen Hell for yourself, re-read the book and then question everything about it, question the lies Tiffany, because it is all lies.' Pushing me through the door he smiles one more time and laughs, 'come back and tell me your findings, we shall have tea next time and discuss your revised opinions of me.'

'Come back to Hell, with the demented Devil? *As if*!'

'Oh I will see you again Tiffany Delamarre, mark my words. You belong down here with me, not up there with the innocent do gooders and you know that you do. And for future reference, my name is Lucifer.'

'Well Lucifer, you can keep Hell, I much prefer Heaven.'

'We shall see.'

His words echo around my brain as I find myself once again in the corridor facing a very angry mob. Myra, Celestia and Daniel do not look pleased to see me.

Heaven and Hell suck!

Chapter Six

'My office now!' Celestia's voice booms around the corridor and Myra has a grin on her face so wide that I fear her face may split. Why am I always in trouble in this place?

Daniel I notice is unusually quiet which puts me on edge a lot more than Celestia's obvious anger. As much as I want to throw my arms around him and enjoy our limited time together, I know that he would not welcome that right now. No doubt I will have to apologise profusely before I even get a smile. I honestly believed that Heaven would be a calming place, happy, delightful, and yet since day one I have been in constant trouble, and let's be straight here, it isn't even my fault normally.

Sure I have messed up on a few occasions, which I have again apologised for, but most of the time I am just trying to help, and Jodie really does need my help!

People are always casting blame in this dump, idiots!

'Fine, fine, whatever!' I grumble as I push past Myra and head towards Celestia's office, might as well as get it over and done with as soon as I can and deal with whatever ridiculous punishment they hand out.

'What in the devil do you think you are playing at?!' Storms Celestia before I have even had a chance to take a seat, 'I mean Hell of all places, are you stupid girl!'

'Have you purposely just made a Devil and Hell reference in the same sentence?' I snigger.

'Shut up Tiff.' Urges Tracey, she looks nervous which in turn makes me nervous. What does she know that I currently do not?

Looking around the room at the red angry faces I suddenly feel incredibly small, like a wriggling bug under a microscope, why are they all looking at me in this manner?

'Once again your immature actions have had serious consequences, not only for Tracey who you have innocently dragged into your mess, but for the whole of Heaven! You do not just pop down to Hell to see the Devil, have you any idea at all of what you have done!'

'I am not innocent in this.' Whispers Tracey, but nobody hears her.

'I did not just pop down to Hell, I had a legitimate reason for it, and if you stopped being so pompous about everything and actually asked me then I could explain it to you.' I snap.

'Unbelievable.' Sighs Myra, 'Is she always like this? So obstinate?'

'Unfortunately yes.' Responds Celestia angrily.

'Then I feel that we have no option but to call in the judges.'

It is like I am no longer in the room, and they call me rude!

'I fear for the repercussions on poor Tracey.' Continues Celestia sadly, 'how can we send her to the judges for something that she clearly wanted no part in.'

'Well we must set an example, this behaviour simply cannot be tolerated.'

'I AM NOT INNOCENT!' yells Tracey, 'ARE YOU DEAF?'

The whole room descends into silence, the Tracey that I know and love has finally returned.

'Do control yourself.' Commands Myra, 'Clearly you are not thinking straight.'

'God give me strength.' She laughs, 'I am as guilty as sin, and if you send Tiff to the cells then you better make sure you send me too, because if you don't....' she pauses, 'then I will make sure everybody here knows just what kind of people you really are! You ask Tiffany to help you and the second she does you screw her over, have you even for a moment considered how she felt going down there? And you Celestia...' She points her finger directly into Celestia's face, 'you know exactly what is going on with this case so how can you stand there and act so high and mighty? Your best friend's daughter is being battered by a scumbag lowlife and instead of supporting Tiff in helping her be free of him, you threaten to have her locked up! I think you all need to get a grip!'

I snigger involuntarily and Daniel shoots me a look of disgust, 'Well she isn't wrong is she.' I snap, 'If you want me punishing then I suggest you call the judges and have me sentenced, I did what was I felt was right and if you cannot handle that then tough! As for you Daniel, what the hell is your problem? I don't see you for ages and when I finally do you give me this attitude! Nice. Well I am through with all of you, I plan to save Jodie without your help and after that I am leaving this dump for good.'

Storming from the room I slam the door and head towards my bedroom. I am going to pack away my belongings and move full time into my City Centre apartment, it has to be better than living here with all of their interchangeable rules and demands. Where I will go when the lease is up I do not know, but it won't be back here that's for sure.

Stuffing clothes and shoes into plastic bags I do not hear Daniel enter the room, my first awareness of him is when he walks up behind me and puts his arms around my waist and apologises for being such a misery.

'Celestia is pretty annoyed.' He says quietly, 'why did you do it?'

'Oh great, not you as well!'

'No, no, look I'm sorry for being grumpy, but when I come home expecting to see you waltzing around the place as you normally do and actually find out that you are in Hell, you have to admit that isn't easy to understand.'

'You could have just asked me, that is all any of you had to do.'

'Okay, well I'm asking you now.'

'Fine. Celestia has me working on this case and it has turned out to be a lot more complex than any of us could have imagined. All I was supposed to do was stop Jodie from going to the spa and having treatment that could harm her, easy enough right? Well no, not really. She has this boyfriend Dwight, a total loser, and he's beating her Daniel, but she's managed to convince herself that he didn't mean to do it, that he's oh so sorry and she won't leave him, in fact she is planning on having the treatment because he wants her to.'

'Right, and how does a day trip to Hell fit into all of this.'

'Because when I went to work at the spa undercover I found out that Juliana was on BFF terms with the owner, so I figured if I went to Hell I could speak with Juliana, find out where the missing owner is hiding, put a stop to the spa once and for all and save Jodie's life. See, not completely insane when you know the full facts is it.'

'Actually...it is pretty insane honey, you went to Hell for crying out loud, how did you even get back? Did you use your wings?'

'Sorry? Wings?' I ask completely puzzled.

'Sure, if you want to travel through different zones you can use your wings to get you out of there, I'm guessing you didn't know this.'

'Actually Maisie mentioned something about wings a while ago; I thought it was just children being silly. And when may I ask do these wings materialise?'

'It generally just happens when you think about it.'

'Great, so I have broken wings as well, does anything ever work in this place?' I fume.

'I'm sure it just takes time, don't stress about it. Seriously though, how did you get out?'

'Lucifer walked me to the door and I left. Simple.'

'Just like that? He didn't ask for anything in return, like your soul?!'

'Oh Daniel please, could you be a little bit more melodramatic! He was the perfect gentleman actually.'

'He is the Devil Tiffany, there is nothing gentlemanly about him, and I want you to stay away from him okay, he is nothing but trouble.'

'Fine, it's not like I ever intend to go there ever again, it was awful.' I shudder at the memory of Juliana and hope that one day I will stop seeing her all cramped up in that dirty little cage.

'So what's it like down there? Did you see Juliana?'

'If it's all the same to you could we talk about this another time? I have had enough Heaven and Hell drama for one day.'

'Sure.' He sounds disappointed that I will not share the Hell tour details, but until I get the screaming out of my mind it is off limits.

'How is your case going?' I ask, 'Are you likely to be home soon?'

'The usual, undercover in a gang that deals drugs.'

'That is the usual? I think you need a change of case.' I laugh.

'No kidding. I shouldn't be much longer with it though, a few weeks maybe.'

'Well I may not be around in a few weeks if Myra has anything to do with it. I cannot believe she wants me locked away until I am judged by this Heavenly Law, what is her problem.'

'You aren't going anywhere, leave Myra and Celestia to me.'

'She seems pretty determined to make an example of me.'

'Trust me okay, it is all going to be fine. You will finish your case, I will finish mine and then we can have a much needed break together, just you and me. So why don't you unpack all of this stuff and stick around?'

'She hates me Daniel so why should I? No matter what I do it is never good enough.'

'Celestia will come around, I will make sure of it.'

'And what about Myra?'

'You leave her to me; I will make sure she never bothers you again. But do me a favour, until I have this sorted out stay away from the corridor.'

I agree that I will stay far away from Myra and the corridor and Daniel assures me that he will smooth things over with Celestia. Tracey was a star standing up for me in there and I hope that she does not get into trouble for it.

Unpacking my things I look around and vow that Jodie will not be coming here any time soon. Dwight is a monster and I fully intend to ensure that the monster is slain.

Chapter Seven

Eerie fog creeps and swirls around me like a cloak, I don't know why I feel in danger, it is like some weird sixth sense which makes me uncertain as to whether the fog is here to hide me from the darkness that chills me so, or to smother me and drag me under into its snapping jaws.

All I do know is that it is cold, so very cold.

My footsteps sound hollow on the pavement, no echo, no click clack of my heels - they are lifeless, like me.

Where am I going? Why am I even out here in this god awful weather? Why is it so silent?

I sense the person before I even hear the footsteps touch the ground behind me, there is most definitely somebody there.

I see a light in the distance and I know that if I can just reach the safety of that light then I will be okay, surely there will be people there, someone, anyone that can help me.

My breath is making little fluffy clouds in the cold night air as I will my legs to move faster, as I beg them to run. Oh why won't they run!

The light is closer now; I can hear voices, happy, relaxed. I am nearly there.

My legs are heavy, like lead weights are strapped to my ankles but I know that I can do this. Reaching out with both arms I begin to cry out for help. As no help materialises I watch in horror as the welcoming light fades away into nothingness.

The footsteps that were chasing me have now caught me

up, and I feel strong man hands snake around my arms as they are pulled sharply behind my back, crying out I beg for him to release me, hot tears streaming down my face as he laughs.

Spinning me around roughly he grabs my face and forces me to look into his eyes, his evil demonic eyes, it is Lucifer that has me, Lucifer that has made me weak and scared, and Lucifer that is leaning in to kiss me.

Pushing with what little strength I have left I force myself away from him, landing heavily on the pavement that not so long ago seemed like my path to safety.

'Get off of me you freak!' I snap whilst trying my best to stand in a dignified manner.

'Oh Tiffany, sweet little Tiffany.' he laughs, 'come with me now, I will take you to your rightful place.'

'And what place would that be you psycho?'

'At my side of course, where else?'

With a whoosh we are gone from the cold city streets, and I am transported very much against my will into the fiery pits of Hell. Great!

'Welcome home Tiffany, please, do take a moment to gather your thoughts.'

I sneer, 'My thoughts are that you better take me back home right now!'

'But you are home, where you belong, with me.' He sounds hurt that I could have it all so wrong, idiot.

'I would rather gouge out my own eyeballs and eat them than spend a lifetime with you! Don't you get it? I hate you, I hate everything that you stand for, you, dear idiotic Lucifer are a loser, and I do not mingle with losers!'

'You dare to speak to me in this manner in my own Kingdom? You dare to throw my hospitality back in my face and look at me with such disdain in your eyes? You think that your precious Daniel is the one for you? Wake up and smell the cinders Tiffany Delamarre, I am bad, you are bad, we are the perfect match.'

'Go to Hell!' I scream in his stupid smirking face.

'Already there baby.' he snarls, 'and until you learn to be a good little girl you will have to pay the consequences of insulting me in my own home.'

'Good little girl? A moment ago you said I was bad.'

'Yes, well you know exactly what I mean.' Clicking his fingers, two huge and quite frankly butt ugly men appear and stand either side of me. 'Take her to the cages; she has some thinking to do.'

'Screw you Lucifer, I will never agree to stay with you, never!'

'Spend a night in my cages, and we will see.'

The cages are as delightful as I remember, *not*!

It would have been bad enough just spending a night in this demented hell hole alone, but just to top it off Lucifer has given me a big fat juicy cherry on top - my cage is right next door to Juliana's.

'Well if it isn't little miss goody two shoes.' she screeches, 'I knew you would fall from grace eventually, nothing but a cheap tacky little tramp.'

'Mmm that really is fascinating coming from the woman that is currently sleeping in her own urine and faeces. Killed any little girls lately?' I smile sweetly.

'It was an accident!'

'Sure it was. I can fully understand how you could accidently launch your little sister off of a mountain and then accidently forget to call mountain rescue. Yes, definitely an accident.'

'Why are you here?' she demands, spittle flying all over the place.

'Because the Devil is in love with me and wants me to spend all of eternity with him.'

'Oh great, sounds about right. Everybody just loves Tiffany Dela-bloody-marre!'

'Whatever Juliana, I won't be here for long, he just needs time to sulk and move the hell on.'

'Ha! The fact that you even think that this is temporary amuses me. He will never let you go, so make yourself comfortable sweetheart, you won't be going anywhere.'

'Oh shut up!'

Settling myself down into the corner far away from anybody that may feel the need to touch me with their grubby hands, I ponder what Juliana has just said. Will I be here forever? Surely Daniel will figure out where I am and save me, won't he?

The screaming starts just as I am nodding off, loud ear piercing screeches that bounce off of the walls and spread like a nasty virus. It doesn't take long for the others to start, Juliana included. I yell for them to stop, I demand to know why they are screaming, but they are possessed, taken over by the noise, they just won't stop.

I put my hands over my ears and pray for the nightmare to end, but it has just begun.

'There she is! Nasty evil bully!' The voice yells over the noise, coming for me. When will I ever be free of my past?

'Get her!'

I watch as they run as fast as their crazed bodies will allow, they show no signs of stopping, faster and faster, do they plan to run right through my cage?!

The screaming becomes more frenzied, cages are rattled so forcefully that I fear they too will come loose and unleash even more haters upon me.

I begin screaming, yelling as hard as my lungs will allow, I beg for help, for mercy, and yet still they come, they want their pound of flesh and I am it!

I recognise them in my terror, all of the people that I have ever hurt and I few that I do not recognise at all, though to be fair that doesn't mean anything, I probably just don't remember them. Why are they coming for me? I have changed, godammit!

'NO!' I scream, 'NO!'

They are upon me, their hands reaching in through the bars, tearing at my bare skin, spitting at me. It won't be long before they have the cage doors open and then I have no doubt at all that I will be torn limb from limb.

Scrabbling as far back as I can go, I curl myself into a little ball and pray for what seems the millionth time that someone will save me. Anyone.

'All you have to do is say the words Tiffany and I will free you.' His words, now like soft velvet against my skin flow gently across the anger and violence aimed solely at me. 'Four tiny little words can end all of this, I.WILL.BE.YOURS. Simple really.'

'Screw you Lucifer, I would rather die! Again!'

'As you wish.'

The door to my cage is flung open and I am dragged from it despite my best attempts to hold tight. Dirty fingers pulling at my hair, kicking me, punching me, is this what I deserve?

Is this really what it felt like to those people that I hurt? Did it feel like this?

Tears hot and fast stream down my cheeks as I try to protect my face and head from my attackers, they are like animals, possessed, demented.

They leave me.

I am bloodied and beaten, my hair bald in places from where they have ripped it so violently from my scalp, my nails broken off in defence of their actions, my body black and blue from the kicks and punches. Do they think that I am dead? Is that why they have gone?

'Four little words Tiffany and I will fix you right back up, as good as new. Deny me again and I will leave them to finish the job that they have started.'

'You.' I spit. Blood drips from my mouth as I speak, 'Send them back in, I will never be with you! Do your worst loser!'

Closing my eyes I feel them descend once more and hope that this time they finish me off. Hands upon my body shaking me, shouting me.

'Tiff, wake up you're having a nightmare. Tiff?'

Tracey's voice reverberates through my brain and even in my sleep like state I know that I am free. Thank God for Tracey Smith, Thank God.

Chapter Eight

Tracey was amazing after my crazy nightmare ordeal. After I had run to the mirror like a woman possessed to check my face was still in one beautiful piece she made me sweet, milky tea, tucked me back up and told me not to worry about a thing, she would always look out for me. I did tell her that it was the Devil himself that was out to get me, but she laughed it off and said she would chase that douche bag moron (her words) right back into the bowels of Hell if she had to.
I just do not know what it is with me and nightmares lately. I know that I was terrible and mean, but I thought that admitting you had a problem was the first step? Or is that just smack heads and alcoholics?
Well either way, my dreams need to cut the crap and get a grip. As for Lucifer... well my plan there is just to stay far away from him and hope he gives up with the chase.
Doubtful, but worth a shot.

Today's agenda is simple. Tracey and I are going to get our smarts on and catch ourselves a 'woman beating, lowlife scumbag, who needs to have his testicles removed with eyebrow tweezers, douche bag'. (Tracey's words again).
Tracey has already set up the meeting. You see while I was getting my face rearranged in my nightmare, Tracey was out reeling Dwayne in. I was a little annoyed with her at first when she told me, but then I remembered she is already dead and I stopped panicking, a bit.
She is meeting him at Bar Salsa at 9pm and I will be

undercover in the lounge area. Dead or not, there is no way I am leaving my friend alone again with that clown.

Jodie was not around when we popped in to see her and let her know of our plan, so we just intend to get it over and done with and then take her out to celebrate.

I have also called in sick at Pearl, I don't want to full on quit the position as it may come in handy at some point, but for now the leads there are nil.

As Tracey emerges from the bedroom I am at a loss for words, unusual I know. She looks stunning. In a tight red dress and matching killer heels there is no way on this planet that Dwight could resist.

'Do I look okay?' she asks me, unsure of the outfit.

'Okay?' I respond laughing, 'You look... and please excuse the pun, drop dead gorgeous! If that loser isn't smitten with you the moment that you walk in then I will happily run around Leeds City Centre completely naked.'

'Well let's hope it doesn't come to that you nutter.' She laughs.

'Come on, let's get this over and done with, I can't wait to tell Jodie that we managed to remove the ball and chain from her ankle once and for all.'

Bar Salsa is heaving but I manage to find a place in the corner where I can see Tracey and the moron. The look on his face screams that all of his Christmases' and birthdays have come at once, whilst Tracey, doing her best to look interested and calm, actually looks petrified.

As Dwight reaches out to touch her leg for the fifth time in as many minutes, Tracey visibly recoils and I feel that we are going to lose this. I watch as he leans in and whispers something into her ear and Tracey's hand curls into a fist, oh god no! She is going to punch him.

Weighing up my options I realise that I actually don't have that many. Dwight has never seen me before so it's not like I will be blowing our cover if I go over there, and let's face it, I am a goddess, how could any man resist.

Fluffing up my already perfect hair I rise gracefully from my seat, take a second to enjoy the admiring glances and make my way over to their table.

'Tracey!' I exclaim in surprise, 'Oh I just knew that it was you, mind if I join you?'

Without waiting for Dwight's response I take a seat, slowly crossing my legs. I do not miss the appreciative glance that he gives my super long pins, gotcha!

'And who is this handsome devil?' I smile seductively at Dwight, despite wanting to throw up my entire lunch, and rake my fingers slowly down his jaw line.

'This is Dwight, my date.' Tracey plays along, 'You don't mind a threeway do you?' she asks bluntly, 'Tiffany and I just love a threeway.'

I can truthfully say that I have never seen a grown man dribble beer, but in slow motion that is precisely what he did. It wasn't a shocked spitting out of beer like in the movies, but an actual dribble. Could this guy be any more pathetic!

'Well... that's a great proposition ladies, but I have to ask, you're not like... well you know...'

He leaves it hanging, and whilst we both know exactly what he means the look that Tracey flashes me says it all... let him say the words.

'Are we what?' Tracey asks innocently.

The silence is heavy, he knows that he has messed up, but

being an arrogant jerk he will go through with the accusation anyway.

Well you know... prozzies?'

'What is a prozzie?' I ask in full virginal mode.

'Oh he means do we have sex with strangers for money.' Clarifies Tracey.

My hand instinctively reaches for my glass of Martini, ready to drown this little cretin, but my brain kicks in and reminds me that that is no way to treat my favourite beverage. Instead I lean towards him and whisper into his ear, 'Do you have a problem with that?'

Again with the dribbling, gross!

'Depends on what you charge sweetheart.' He drawls.

Now, my knowledge of prostitutes is limited I have to say, Other than watching reruns of Band of Gold I have zero expertise in this field. Picking up on my floundering Tracey marches on in with a full price list and graphic details of our 'services'. I am shocked. How could my lovely little Tracey know so much about this? I make a mental note to have a little chat with her about her activities before she died.

'That sounds right up my street.' Dwight smirks, 'You have a place in mind?'

'We sure do, but we have some rules before we get started.' She continues.

'Fine, anything you say darlin'.'

Again I sit shocked and entranced as Tracey reels off a list of rules as long as your arm.

No kissing on the lips / No kinky stuff / payment up front, that kind of thing. Wow!

Draining his drink he makes some remark about taking a whizz and says he will be right back.

'Oh my god Tracey, now what?' I ask truly terrified at the thought of going anywhere with this creep.

'Now we play him at his own game.' She smiles, 'And I have the perfect place.'

Fifteen minutes and a lot of inappropriate comments and touching later we pull up in Dwight's car outside of an old abandoned mill. I asked Tracey how she knew about such a place and all she said was that she had friends on the game and this would be the perfect place.

Looking around and being thankful that I am already deceased (this is a murderer's paradise) I watch as Tracey takes the lead and directs Dwight towards a flight of stairs. The building smells of urine and burnt rubber and is dark as Hell. I hope Tracey knows what she is doing.

'This way' she purrs, 'not long now.'

I hear a zipper being tugged down and pray that this does not end badly; I have never felt so tainted in my whole life. Taking a deep breath I stand behind Dwight and slowly begin to remove his shirt, his groan of excitement repulses me.

'You like being handcuffed big boy?' Tracey asks him confidently.

'Whatever bitch, whatever!' he practically yells, 'Just get on with it.'

Removing handcuffs from god knows where, Tracey slowly handcuffs Dwight to the rickety drainpipe behind me, at least now he can't touch us anymore.

Going slow to her knees Tracey tugs at Dwight's jeans until they are pooled around his ankles, oh my god, please tell me she isn't go to... this needs to stop, now!

I am reaching out to grab her when I see that she is

actually tying his ankles together.

'There we go.' She laughs, 'all secure now.'

'Well... get on with it!' he demands.

'Get on with what?' she asks.

'You damn well know what I mean woman.'

'You know Dwiiiight.' She drags his name out slowly, 'you really should be careful who you pick up in bars, I mean, what would your girlfriend say?'

'I don't have a girlfriend.' He denies vehemently.

'Oh? So the name Jodie means nothing to you?' I demand.

'What?' he splutters.

'Yep, we know all about Jodie you cheating pig.' Taking her phone from her little clutch bag, Tracey takes a photo and promises him that if he even so much as looks at Jodie again the photo will go viral. I am impressed.

'You can't do this!' he screams, 'Untie me now!'

'We can do whatever the hell we like sweetheart.' I grin.

'You can't leave me here!'

'Oh, I know this area really well.' Giggles Tracey, 'Trust me you'll have company soon enough.'

As we walk away arm in arm I can't help but wonder what will happen to Dwight, then I realise that I do not care. I hope that whoever does turn up here tonight enjoys our little gift; I just wish that we had a bow, then he would have been gift wrapped and ready to party.

Oh well, you can't have everything. Good luck Dwight, you are going to need it.

Chapter Nine

Knocking on Jodie's door we giggle even more with the absurdity of what we have just done. It is midnight and whilst I feel a little terrible for getting Jodie up, I know that she rarely sleeps anyway as I have heard her pacing around her apartment late at night. Probably worried that loser is going to break in or something.

'Guys?' Mumbles Jodie, rubbing tired eyes and blinking herself into focus, 'is everything okay?'

'Oh Jodie.' Laughs Tracey, 'It was so perfect, you should have seen us, you should have seen him!'

'Okaaaay, what on earth are you on about?' She asks, clearly confused.

'Dwight of course. We got him good Jodie; he won't be bothering you again.'

Her hands fly to her face as she instantly looks horrified. 'Oh girls, what have you done? What have you done?' The tears begin slowly at first, quickly turning into a full blown monsoon. 'What have you done, oh god, he'll kill me!'

Taking her by the hands we steer her towards the sofa and sit her down.

'C'mon love, he can't hurt you anymore now, we made sure of that.' Soothes Tracey.

Taking a deep breath she looks at us both in turn and shakily asks us exactly what we did.

As I explain as best as I can, in a way that will not alarm her even further, Tracey busies herself in the kitchen making sweet tea for everyone. Tracey is obsessed with sweet tea.

Jodie's response is not at all what we predicted. Throwing herself from the sofa she rushes to the door mumbling to herself that she must help him, she must save him.

To say that myself and Tracey were easily strong enough to stop her would be a lie. A woman on a mission it would seem is stronger than a bear.

Finally managing to restrain her and lock her in her bedroom, we lean against the door panting heavily, this was so not the way that I had expected this evening to end. I had expected triumph, happiness, and celebrations. Not anger and a rather strange urgency to help the man that beats you senseless at the drop of a hat.

'Let me out!' screams Jodie from behind the bedroom door, 'Let me out or so help me god I will climb through this bloody window!'

'We are on the top floor Jodie, don't be ridiculous.'

'Are you mocking me?' She demands to know. 'Let's see how much mocking you'll be doing when he comes back and kills me!'

'He is not going to kill you, I doubt after tonight he would dare to even come near you ever again. Trust us Jodie; we did you a massive favour tonight.' Declares Tracey, proudly.

We are met with silence.

'Erm... Jodie? You are still in there, right?' I ask nervously. Surely she wouldn't have climbed out of the window, would she?

'Of course I'm in here! Like a bloody prisoner in my own home, not that it will matter much when he gets free, I'll be dead anyway.'

'Look.' I begin, slowly losing patience, 'Dwight is no good for you, and deep down you know that. He had you signed up for cosmetic surgery for crying out loud, seriously Jodie you need to cut this loser loose!'

'Yeah well don't think I don't know that you had something to do with my appointment being cancelled, because I do. I don't know how you did it, but stop interfering! I was managing perfectly well before you came along.'

'Oh really!' I snap, beyond irritated now. 'Managing perfectly well with a massive bruise on your face? Sure, sounds like you were doing just great! Get a grip Jodie; he would have killed you by now if it hadn't been for us!'

'Well guess what? He's going to kill me now anyway, so I guess your whole plan just totally went tits up! Well done!'

'I swear to...' Tracey shushes me as I once again begin to rant, and suggests that I go and make more tea. 'Fine, you deal with the deluded one!'

Pottering about in the kitchen I calm down somewhat and begin to ponder the situation. Maybe we have done more harm than good. Maybe Jodie is right.

The man clearly has issues, he most certainly cannot contain his anger, and what do we do? We put him in a situation that will no doubt further fuel his crazed fire.

Have I messed up yet again?

Pouring the tea I make yet another vow that I will put this right. Just how many times have I had to do this since dying... too many.

'Tiff?' Jodie's voice is croaky from crying and shouting, 'Tiff I'm sorry, I know that you were both just doing what you thought was right, and I appreciate it, really I do. But you don't know Dwight, not like I do. He will come for me, not right away, but he will.'

'We will protect you, you know that.'

'What? Night and day? He will wait, until I feel safe and secure again, until I feel for certain that he is gone, and then there he will be. Watching, waiting. I've seen the darkness in him, trust me, he will be coming for me.'

Tracey has released Jodie from her boudoir prison and she looks exhausted.

'Then move in with me.'

'That won't solve anything. He isn't stupid, he will just wait until I am alone and then strike.'

'You can't live in fear of this loser Jodie, you just can't.'

'What choice do I have? He wants me and there is nothing that I can do about it. Please tell me where he is so that I can go and try to put things right. Maybe if I get to him first, apologise, he won't be so brutal.'

'Not a chance in hell honey.' Pipes up Tracey, 'this douche bag does not own you, he does not rule your life, you do, and so help me god I will kill him if he so much as lays a finger on you.'

Sighing Jodie flops down onto the sofa and buries her head into the cushion, the tears once again flowing freely. I just do not know what to do.

Looking at Tracey I shrug my shoulders in helplessness, and she winks at me. Turning towards Jodie's laptop that is open and turned on she quickly types something into the search engine and music fills the quiet room.

I know this song!

The First Wives Club, Bette Midler, Goldie Hawn, Diane Keaton! The perfect choice.

As Tracey begins singing I can't help but join in...Could there be a more fitting song right now? Doubtful.

Flinging our arms in the air and dancing around the room like lunatics we sing the song to Jodie with all of our might.

You don't own me
I'm not just one of your many toys
You don't own me
Don't say I can't go with other boys

Don't tell me what to do
And don't tell me what to say
And when I go out with you
Don't put me on display

You don't own me...

As the music comes to a sudden halt and myself and Tracey are left screeching like banshees, Jodie's little voice echoes around the now silent room.
'You're wrong. Dwight does own me.'

Chapter Ten

The night was long and draining as we tried to make Jodie understand that Dwight does not own her and that we will protect her from him.

Eventually she fell asleep and we took this as our cue to stand guard at her door.

The night remained uneventful, no sign of pervy Dwight anywhere, which was a huge relief to us both. Had he turned up, despite our intentions to protect Jodie I fear that we would not have been strong enough to keep him from her. Though we would have given it our all.

Jodie ushered us out this morning with a smile and a wave, saying that a good night's sleep had done her the world of good and that she was now feeling much better about things.

We both knew that she was lying, but decided not to push our luck.

Tracey has headed to bed, and I wish that I could do the same. I feel exhausted. But I have a lot to do and no time to spare.

I am still no closer to finding the owner of Pearl and I have absolutely no leads to follow whatsoever. Juliana was a complete waste of time, and I wish so much that I had Daniel here with me to discuss things with.

Celestia of course is my other option, but we didn't exactly leave things in a good way the last time that we saw each other. I know that I am going to have to face her at some point, but I would rather that point be when I have some solid good news for her.

'You could always ask me you know.'

Spinning around I am alarmed to see Lucifer lounging all the way across my Laura Ashley sofa as though he has every right to be there.

'What the hell do you want?' I demand to know instantly.

'Ha, nice. I came to offer my assistance to a very beautiful damsel in distress,'

'yes, well I am neither in distress, nor am I a damsel, so get your grubby body off of my designer settee before I hurt you.'

'Like you did to poor Dwight' He laughs and it sends chills through my body.

'And what would you know about that?'

'I watched the entire spectacle unfold, it was truly magnificent, would you like all of the gory details? I stayed right until the end of the show, so I have them all.'

'Is he... erm...?'

'Dead? No of course not, where would be the fun in that. I released him right after the hookers had a good laugh.'

'Did they do... erm... did they harm him?'

'Would it please you if they had?'

'Yes actually it would!' I snap, defiantly.

'They did nothing; they had other interests to take care of at the time.' He winks and I gag.

I feel slightly nauseas at the thought of Lucifer witnessing our actions last night, and hope that he does not take it as the dark side that he seems convinced that I have.

'You made quite the convincing lady of the night, though your friend, Tracey isn't it? She was wonderful.'

'You know damn well that her name is Tracey, and I am warning you right now to stay away from her!'

Stalking towards me he whispers softly into my ear, 'you

know that it is only you that I want Tiffany.'

Pushing past him I stand behind the coffee table, more comfortable with this temporary fort between us. 'Did you not understand me the last time we met? I am not interested.'

'Yes, more interested in the rather dashing Daniel Fox.'

'You...'

'I know, I know, stay away from him too. I am almost tempted to do the exact opposite just to see what you would do. It would be interesting, do you not agree?'

'No I do not agree. What do you want Lucifer?'

'Other than you? I am only here to offer my assistance. Juliana was unforthcoming, a disappointment and setback for you no doubt. Let me help you Tiffany Delamarre, it would be my absolute pleasure.'

'I do not need any help.'

'Oh, know where the owner of Pearl Beauty Spa is then, do you?'

'You know damn well that I do not!'

'Then why are you so reluctant to accept my help?'

'Because you have an ulterior motive, that is why.'

'Which is?'

'How the hell do I know!' I fume, 'You are sneaky and underhanded, and god only knows what goes on in that head of yours.'

He laughs, 'Even God does not know the answer to that.'

'Whatever! Just stay away from me, okay.'

'It will not be long before you need me. I am a patient man, but I am yet undecided as to whether or not I will make you beg for my help.'

'Dream on!' I snort, 'Tiffany Delamarre begging for help? *As if*!'

With a whoosh he is gone, his laughter echoing long after his vanishing act. What a loser!

'Hey what's with the shouting?'

Tracey looks as cute as anything in her little chemise, which makes me extra happy that she did not come out looking like that whilst Lucifer was here.

'Oh you know, just the Devil himself invading my privacy.'

'What? He was here? And I missed him?'

'Be thankful, the guy is a first class cretin.'

'Eww I didn't mean it like that Tiff, it just would have been cool to go back and tell Caleb that I met the Devil... and that I kicked his arse all the way back to Hell.'

Laughing I pass Tracey a cup of her favourite... ridiculously sweet tea and fill her in on what Lucifer wanted, and the fact that he was watching us last night.

'Too creepy.' She shudders. 'Has he really got it that bad for you?'

'Seems to have.' I sigh, 'I just want to see Daniel, it feels like forever.'

'Yeah, I wouldn't mind having some alone time with Caleb, if you know what I mean!'

'So, head up there now and spend the day with him, I can guard Jodie's door.'

'And what if the douche bag makes an appearance?' She asks, concerned.

'Then I will... no idea, I'll have to wing it.' I shrug.

'Nope, not good enough, I'll stay.'

'You are a good friend Tracey Smith, do you know that.'

'Good? I know for a fact that you meant to say amazingly fab right there in the good section!'

'That I did.' I reply laughing, 'That is exactly what I

meant.'

'You know.' Tracey begins after a moment, 'you could accept Lucifer's help.'

'What! Are you nuts?'

'No, no, hear me out. He has a lot of connections, he could source out the info we need in a heartbeat, then you just sack him off and forget all about him.'

'Wow, Tracey, look I don't think people get to just sack off the Devil. If he helps me then I can bet my entire collection of Louboutins that he will want the favour returning.'

'But not if you set ground rules first.'

'Trust me, Lucifer does not follow rules, he makes his own as he goes along. I am just not prepared to play against the Devil, something tells me he plays dirty.'

'I guess you're right, just a thought.'

'We will find her, and when we do we will make sure she shuts Pearl and never harms another woman again. Until then however we need to protect Jodie. So, do you want to check on her first or shall I?'

Tracey ponders this for a moment and then pulls out a coin. 'We'll flip for it.'

I choose tails as not going first and am instantly disappointed to see the Queen staring at me from Tracey's hand.

'Good luck kiddo, you'll need it.' She laughs hysterically as I make my way out of the apartment. Great! Here's hoping the hysterics have stopped.

Knocking I wait impatiently for the door to be answered. Good luck indeed.

'Oh hey Tiff.' Jodie looks pale and unrested. 'I didn't expect to see you again today.'

'I couldn't leave things as they were yesterday without us talking, are we okay?' I ask.

'Sure, sure.' She waves her hand flippantly and tries to close the door in my face.

'Are you sure that everything is okay? You seem a little jittery.'

'Wouldn't you be if your crazed ex was on the loose?'

'I am so sorry to ask this Jodie, but... he isn't in there is he? Are you hiding him? You really need to get your priorities straightened out if you are!'

She recoils from me as though I have slapped her.

'You think after everything that you guys did for me last night I would just take him back? I would hide him away in here like a dirty little secret away from my friends? You just don't have a clue do you Tiffany! You may have no idea what it is like to be a loyal friend but I do, and I would never betray you or Tracey like that. Maybe it's you that needs to get their priorities straight Tiffany, because mine are just fine!'

'Jodie I...' The door is slammed in my face and I sink to the ground in despair.

I have blown it again. When will I learn to keep my big mouth shut!

Chapter Eleven

Daniel has returned and he has proposed to me!

I had returned to Heaven in the hope of speaking with Celestia about the Jodie / Pearl situation, but found her deep in conversation with evil Myra. I decided not to make my presence known as the woman clearly despises me, and to be perfectly honest I was not in the mood for a confrontation with her.

Jodie would not open the door to me again yesterday, she just continually shouted through it that I needed to revaluate my life and to go back and see her when I had a clue who I was.

Easier said than done when you are Tiffany Delamarre, bully turned hopeful good girl.

Anyway, there I was undecided as to my next action when Daniel appeared out of nowhere, picked me up, spun me around, kissed me, put me down and then dropped to one knee. To say that I was surprised would be a major understatement.

Of course I accepted, I would be a fool not to.

So here we are lazing about in the gardens and I have the biggest diamond on my finger known to man. Bliss? I wish. I should be revelling in my engagement, excited at the prospect of planning our wedding, and yet here I am sullen and distant. Damn you Jodie!

'Hey.' Daniel nudges me, 'You seem a little depressed for a recently engaged woman.'

Sitting up I face my fiancé, oh yes, and take his hand. 'I have done something bad Daniel.'

'What? You? Never!' he laughs.

'I mean it, I have messed up again, why do I keep doing this?'

'Tell me what you've done and I'll see if I can help.' He smiles.

I explain in great detail all about Jodie and Dwight, about Tracey and I pretending to be prostitutes and leaving Dwight handcuffed to a drainpipe. I tell him all about Jodie's reaction and the Devil appearing to me, and then I tell him how I accused my new friend of deceiving me. I leave nothing out.

'Seems to me like you were just being a good friend honey, give her time, she'll come around.'

'Am I a good friend though? Do friends accuse their friends of lying and keeping secrets?'

'Well, no. But good friends do look out for each other and that is all that you were doing. Why don't you go around there, explain how you feel and take it from there.'

'She won't see me.' I sulk. 'She said I need to revaluate my life.'

'I'm sure she didn't mean it.' He pulls me into a hug, 'Give it another go, okay?'

'Sure, but it won't do any good'

'Okay, for the next hour you are not allowed to be sad or grumpy about anything, we just got engaged Tiff, be a little happy.'

Feeling instantly bad that I have put a downer on our engagement I push Jodie to the back of my mind and snuggle in closer to my husband to be.

'So why the sudden proposal anyway?' I ask, curious as to his motive.

'Would because I love you sound like a decent answer?'

he chuckles.

'Obviously it would, but I know you, so spit it out.'

'This case has really gotten to me Tiff, made me realise a few things about myself, about where I want to be. I have seen families torn apart during this undercover work, and it's made me see that yes I love you, and yes we are together, but I want more. I want us to be properly together, you and me, forever.'

'We definitely have the forever part sorted.'

'We certainly do.'

'Hey you two love birds, get a room!' Victoria's voice booms across the gardens and as I wave hello she instantly sees the sparkle from my diamond ring. 'Well, well, well.' She screeches, 'congratulations!'

As Maisie and Sophie come running over to see what all of the fuss is about I can't help but feel that I am finally home. I am at last where I deserve to be, with the people that I deserve to be with. Of course it sucks that I have to be dead to have all of this, but who cares, when I was alive I was never truly living anyway.

'When is the big day then?' asks Victoria, 'When do I need to get a hat for?'

'Oh not for a while yet I should think.' I answer, mind far away on bridal gowns and flower girls, 'I need time to plan and organise.'

'If you know Tiff like I do then this wedding will be a masterpiece.'

'Can we be bridesmaids?' asks Maisie, pointing to herself and Sophie.

'I would love it if you would be my bridesmaids.' I reply, scooping them both up. 'I would love it more than anything in the entire universe.'

'More than you love Daniel?' squeaks Sophie.

'Erm...'

'Tiffany there you are, moment of your time if you would.' Saved by the bell, or rather the evil corridor monitor. What now?

'I am rather busy at the moment Myra, it will have to wait.' I respond snootily.

'No, it will be now, come along.' She begins marching away and I can feel the old Tiffany Delamarre itching to break free, I try to restrain her, really I do, but she is too strong.

'I said no!'

She turns to face me, her face ashen, eyes bulging. 'Do not disobey me.' She growls.

'Listen moron, you don't tell me what I can and cannot do, so why don't you run along back to your boring corridor and contemplate getting a grip!'

'You will come with me now!' she yells across the serene landscape.

'And you will go to Hell. I've been, it would suit you nicely, lots of other nut jobs for you to play with.'

'Celestia is going to hear about this insubordination.'

'Does my face look even remotely interested?'

'It should do, I am going to personally bring you down Tiffany Delamarre, you should be worried. I am going to make your existence a nightmare!'

'Oh hardly! I've lived through nightmares, and you don't even scratch the surface of that title. Now get lost, I am celebrating with my friends.'

'I will make you pay Tiffany, you will burn in Hell for this.'

'No, I will be planning my wedding, and it's going to be

the wedding of all weddings. Don't wait by the door for your invitation, it won't be coming.'

'And you will not be getting married. Its law, didn't you know?' She smirks.

'Oh joy, another one of your stupid rules. Really Myra you should know better than to try and stop me from doing anything, you won't win.'

'Heavenly Law is not stupid, as you will very soon be finding out.'

'Did you just threaten me?' I demand to know.

'No threats, only promises.' She walks away, leaving me reeling, is she going to have me brought up on some fictitious charge?

Is that why she was speaking so privately with Celestia? 'Don't worry about that old hag.' Soothes Victoria, 'she has no power in this place, only Celestia can make decisions like that.'

'I'm not exactly Celestia's favourite person right now, after the whole breaking and entering debacle.'

'You leave both of them to me.' Fumes Daniel, 'and do not fret your pretty little head.'

'She makes me so angry, where has she even come from anyway? One minute the corridor runs itself, the next the gatekeeper from Hell appears. Very bizarre.'

'Indeed, and I plan to find out just who this Myra is.'

'Just be careful okay, she seems intent on having someone charged with... well anything.'

'I will be perfectly careful, but you stay out of her way for now, do not give her any reason to stir up an argument that she can use against you.'

'I'm going back to Earth anyway to solve this Pearl situation and make amends with Jodie, so she will have no reason to charge me with anything, because I won't be here.'

'Good good. Now, I have to get back to the case, but I want you to do something for me.'

'Sure, anything?'

'Go and party, celebrate our good news, have a fantastic time, and then I'll be home before you know it.'

Kissing Daniel goodbye and promising him that I would celebrate our wonderful news in style was difficult. How could I celebrate without him?

It's time to put this case to bed and sort out my life (okay, death).

First things first, put a stop to this evil Detox centre. Pearl will shine no more.

Chapter Twelve

Apologising to Jodie in the end wasn't so difficult. She had calmed down immeasurably and I apologised until I was out of breath from talking. A first for me I must admit. Now, Tracey, Jodie and I are slowly getting drunk in my apartment to celebrate my engagement to the seriously delicious Daniel Fox.

OMG I am engaged!

I am engaged to a man that I once thought was a stalker killer. *Nice.*

'Hey Tiff, you aren't gonna turn into Bridezilla are you?' asks Tracey worriedly.

'Bride what?' I question. 'What on earth is that?'

'That's where you go all schizo and start bossing people around and being a general pain in the arse.' She smiles, 'Oh wait, that's you anyway... never mind.'

Throwing a cushion at her face I look around me and suddenly realise that this is my first ever sleep over, with actual real friends. Wow!

'I'm so jealous Tiff.' Sniffs Jodie, 'I wish I could find a guy that would love me like Daniel loves you. Do you think Dwight could ever...?'

'Hell no!' Tracey yells, sloshing wine all over the kitchen floor, 'If you ever think about marrying that guy then I will... well I don't know what I'll do, but it won't be pretty!'

'He could change.'

Here we go again; I just do not know what to do with Jodie. Why is she so obsessed with this creep?

'You will find somebody eventually that is perfect for you.' I soothe, 'Somebody that won't ever use your face as a punch bag, okay? Now forget about that pleb, we have some serious drinking to do.'

Whoop whoops ring out around the apartment, Tracey puts on some music and before we know it the party is in full swing. Tracey is bouncing around on my ridiculously expensive settee, I am trying my hardest not to tell her to get the hell off, and Jodie is spinning around in circles singing her little heart out to Kylie Minogue. I hope that she doesn't vomit.

'Sambuca anyone?' Shouts Tracey.

I am just about to nod my agreement when my mobile phone starts ringing. Moving away from the party I look at the screen and read the display – Lab geeks – Wonder what they want?

'Hello?'

'Yo Tiff.' It's Johnny one of the laboratory technicians, otherwise known as a lab geek. 'Report is in on your messed up facial creams, man it's bad!'

'I know that it is bad Johnny, that is why it is killing people. So, what do you have?'

'Formaldehyde.' He says simply.

'Excuse me?'

'For-mal-de-hyde. It is used in the art of embalming, you know, on dead people.'

'And what exactly does it do?' And gross!

'It preserves the body, well long enough for loved ones to come and view it anyway. Look, this is serious stuff Tiff; it's incredibly strong, stinks to high heaven and trust me when I say you do not want this anywhere near your skin or innards. Its sick man!'

'What would it take to kill somebody with this stuff Johnny?'

'Not a lot! All this so called beauty place has to do is use a decent dosage and it will quite easily snuff someone out. As for it being in the creams, well...'

'What kind of dosage are we talking about here?'

'Let me put it this way for you... if you ingested a 1oz water solution that contains 37% formaldehyde you would more than likely die. Listen, ingesting less than that can cause all sorts of nasties to happen... convulsions, respiratory failure... the list of delights is endless. If the respiratory failure doesn't get you, then you can bet ya bottom dollar that the severe corrosion of your gastrointestinal tract will finish you off. Nice or what?! Now imagine that solution in an actual Detox drink? Or even that percentage in a face cream.'

'Jesus Johnny! Why would somebody use something so lethal in a beauty product? And how the hell do I stop her?'

'I dunno, maybe in some twisted way she feels if it preserves the dead it can preserve the living also, as for stopping her, I don't know the answer to that Tiff, but I suggest you do it quickly.'

'Thank you Johnny. Does anybody else know about the report yet?'

'Nah, thought I'd hit you with the crap news first, you wanna tell everyone else?'

'If that would be okay? I have somebody that I would like to consult with before I do.'

'Oh? My review of the situation not good enough?' He chuckles.

'You know it is, but this other guy, well let's just say he

has the kind of inside information that I require right now.'
'Good luck, your gonna need it on this one.

Cutting the party short didn't go down too well with the girls at first, but when I explained I had an emergency at the funeral home they understood. Sort of.

Jodie decided to sit this one out; she said that it sounded too morbid and disturbing. Tracey on the other hand was raring to go. Freak.

So here I am, once again standing outside of Damien Kernick's funeral home in the dead of night. Marvellous!

'Tiffany Delamarre as I live and breathe, do you ever sleep?'

'I'm dead Damien, do you?'

'I live and work with the dead Tiffany, it's nearly the same thing.'

'Hardly! But okay. Can we come in?'

Ushering us into the lounge area Damien looks me up and down and says that death still agrees with me, I do not disagree, obviously I look amazing.

'Is your friend here dead also?' he enquires curiously.

'Tracey, nice to meet you.' She extends her hand which Damien takes gently.

'The pleasure is all mine.' He drawls. Eww gross!

'Okay, okay, get a grip on yourself. I need your help and I need it fast.'

'Well I didn't think it would just be a social call. Never do get social calls these days.'

'Mmm can't imagine why.'

'Tea?' he asks, ignoring my comment.

'No, thanks. Look I need information on Formaldehyde,

can you help?'

'I think it may be a little too late in proceedings for you to be embalmed Tiffany dear.'

'Funny! I need to know where it can be bought from, is there like a main supplier or something?'

'A main supplier? I do not understand.'

'What Tiff is trying to say...' interrupts Tracey, '...is, if say I wanted to pop down to the shops and buy myself a whole barrel of formaldehyde to maim and kill people with, where would I go?'

'Is that your intention girls?' he asks warily, 'because if it is...'

'Of course it isn't you nitwit!' I snap angrily, 'We need to know because somebody is using this in a range of beauty products that they are selling and people are dying, so please, Damien, where can this stuff be purchased from?'

'Anywhere.'

'What do you mean anywhere?'

'Online, funeral trades people, black market, dark web, if you want Formaldehyde then trust me; you can source it just about anywhere.'

'Great!'

'You know at one time drug addicts believed that dipping joints or cigarettes into Formaldehyde would get them high, utterly ridiculous of course, Formaldehyde has zero drug value, which probably explains why funeral homes and morgues are not burgled for it.'

'So there is no way for me to track this down?' I ask wearily. 'I wouldn't have thought so. If it is being used in cosmetics, then it will be being used illegally, the chances of locating the supplier would be slim to none I'm afraid.'

Leaving Damien's we take a taxi back home and find Jodie fast asleep on the settee cuddling a very nearly empty bottle of red wine, I guess she finally found a way to sleep. I just hope that Dwight stays far away from her now; the poor girl has been through enough.

Sliding onto one of the bar stools in the kitchen I look over at Tracey, 'We need to find the owner of Pearl, without her we are stumped.'

'Yeah, but where do we start? Juliana was no help when you visited her, the girl in the shop was useless and the Devil is most definitely a no go.'

'I have no idea.' I yawn.

'Get to bed okay, maybe a good night's sleep will help one of us figure out where to go next. There has to be a solution Tiff.'

'I hope so, I really do.'

Flopping onto my bed I close my eyes and instantly feel myself drifting away.

I have no choice now. I need Celestia's help.

Chapter Thirteen

Taking a deep breath I push open the door to Celestia's office and I am thankful to find that mental Myra is nowhere to be seen.

Celestia looks tired and not at all pleased to see me, which has me instantly on guard.

'Hi.' I say tentatively.

She looks up from her paperwork and rubs her sleepy eyes, she does not smile.

'Tiffany, please... take a seat.'

She waits for me to sit down before she begins speaking again, this time more animated and more like her old self.

'I hear that you have had yet another run in with Myra! Just what is your problem with authority Tiffany?'

'Excuse me?'

'Myra requested your presence yesterday and you were as I understand purposely obnoxious.'

'Obnoxious? She never requested my presence at all, she demanded it! Since when does she have the right to demand anything of me?!'

'I required your presence yesterday and I asked Myra to collect you.'

'Well in future if you need to see me then I suggest you come and get me yourself!'

Standing and moving around the desk towards me she frowns, 'I had thought that we were over all of this bad attitude towards others, and yet here you are again deliberately disobeying orders, shouting your mouth off and being rude, and quite frankly I am tired of it.'

'You are tired of it? Try being me!'

'Why are you here Tiffany?'

'I came to tell you that the report on Pearl came in last night, evidently that was a mistake.'

'If it came in last night then why am I only hearing about it now?' She demands.

'Are you for real?' I ask furiously. 'Last night I was speaking with Damien Kernick in relation to the Formaldehyde that has been found in the drinks and the creams used at Pearl. I wanted to gather as much information as I could before I came and spoke with you today. Maybe just maybe if you and super Myra weren't so joined at the hip you would have an actual clue as to what has been going on in this case!'

'How dare you!'

'No! How dare you! I work my bloody hardest to please you, always trying to please you, and for what? For you to throw it back in my face at every opportunity. Well screw you Celestia. I am going to finish this case and then I want no more, do you hear me? No more!'

'I am removing you from the case, with immediate effect.'

'You can't do that.'

'I just did.' She snarls.

'Then I will continue without your authorisation or your support, you just try and stop me!'

Ignoring my last comment she makes her way back around the desk and picks up the telephone. 'Bring her in.' she commands of the person on the receiving end.

'Bring who in?' I enquire.

As the door swings open I am faced with Myra and one very very angry Tracey Smith.

'She just came and grabbed me Tiff, right from your

apartment.'

'What is going on here? I demand to know right this instance!' I yell.

Pushing Tracey further into the room Myra takes centre stage and grins manically at us both. 'Tiffany Delamarre and Tracey Smith, you are hereby called to the courts under the rules of Heavenly Law. You will be judged in accordance with this law, and should you be found to be guilty you will be sentenced to an eternity in Limbo. Do you understand?'

'Oh my god you have got to be kidding me! Celestia are you really doing this? Are you having us judged?'

Celestia does not look up from her desk and her words are barely audible as she instructs Myra to take us to the cells.

'I hope you burn in hell Celestia, I hope you burn real bad!' I scream.

The cells are not as bad as I had imagined. They are a world away from the cells in Hell, but they are cells none the less.

'Let me out this instance!' I demand to thin air, 'You cannot keep us locked up in here! I demand to speak with a lawyer!'

'It's no use Tiff, I don't think anybody is out there.'

'How could she? How could she sit there and just agree to this?' I fume.

'I don't know, but that sneaky cow Myra has a lot to with it.'

'Do you think she has something over Celestia?'

'Possibly, but who knows what, I always thought she was whiter than white.'

'Evidently not. I wish Daniel was here, he would know

what to do.'

'He is certainly gonna be narked off when he finds out we are in here.'

Standing I rattle the cell bars again 'I demand my one phone call! You can't just leave us here with nothing, you are breaking the law!'

'What do you think will happen to us?' Tracey sounds so little and scared.

'Limbo allegedly, though god only knows what that means.'

'It's a world between worlds, a nothing land, just full of sad, lonely people that have nowhere real to be. I don't think I can be one of those people Tiff.'

'You won't be.' I reassure her, 'we are getting out of here, we have done nothing wrong.'

'I see you are settling in just fine, however if you could please stop rattling the bars.'

Myra has the biggest smirk on her face and I want to slap it from her with all that I have.

'Why are you doing this?' cries Tracey, 'why?'

'Because she's a complete loser Tracey that has no friends and seriously no sense of style, she needs to find a way to have some control so she picks on innocent people.'

'Why, you made me sound a little like you.' she grins.

'Hardly! Considering you dress like a vagrant and I do not.'

'If all that separates us is our individual taste in clothes then yes Tiffany, I do believe that you are exactly like me.'

'Taste? Seriously! Dream on. You know that whatever this is it isn't going to stick, you have nothing on us.'

'Oh I do believe that breaking into Hell and conversing with the Devil is a pretty big issue.'

'So are those shoes!' I snigger.

'Laugh all you wish, tomorrow you will be judged and I will be there to witness you being removed from Heaven once and for all. You are a trouble maker Tiffany, and I do not tolerate trouble makers in my Heaven.'

'Ah, at last your true motives make an appearance. You want Celestia's job, makes perfect sense now. And what is to stop me from mentioning that tomorrow in court?'

'Who would believe you? A woman that conspires with the Devil himself?'

'You won't get away with this.'

She ignores me and looks over at a deflated and defeated Tracey, 'You know Tracey, you wouldn't have been in this mess if you had stayed away from her.' She spits, 'But now she has dragged you down with her, such a shame. Though maybe you could plead that you were forced into it, I am sure with Tiffany's background it would be believable.'

Standing Tracey makes her way over to Myra, wipes the tears from her eyes and smiles, 'I would rather suffer everyday for all of eternity than betray my best friend, so why don't you do us all a favour and jog on!'

'As you wish, silly child.'

'I'm sorry Tiff, I've been sat there moping like a right idiot, but I'm done with that now, so how's about we figure a way out of this mess?'

'Did you just say that I'm your best friend?'

'Yeah, you got a problem with that Barbie?'

'Nope.' I smile.

'Good!'

'So, bestie.' I grin, 'What is the plan?'

'Er... I thought maybe you would have one.'

'We know that Myra wants Celestia's position in Heaven right, so, tomorrow when we are called we tell the judges that, explain how she has been with everybody, the changes that she has made and hope that they believe us.'

'They might look at the changes as a good thing. If it stops people from breaking into Hell.'

'Mmm good point. I guess all we have then is praying that Daniel comes home soon and talks some sense into Celestia.'

'Or, that Celestia comes to her senses by herself, hopefully by tomorrow morning.'

'We need a miracle, plain and simple.

Chapter Fourteen

'All rise, this court is now in session. The Honourable Judge Freeman presiding.'
There is silence throughout the court as Judge Freeman takes his place and looks down upon us. I have never felt so nervous in my entire life. Tracey sitting beside me is visibly shaking, but the determined look upon her face tells me that she will not take this lying down.
Beside Judge Freeman (his name must be a joke) are two of the scariest looking women I have ever come across. If they are the ones to sentence us then we are doomed.
The court room is small, almost claustrophobic, and everything is brown. *Yuk*!
Myra is sitting two seats to our left and she looks as though she has won already, well we won't be going down without a fight!
We refused a lawyer in the end as we were not sure that they could be trusted. This whole thing has been a farce since the beginning and we really do not need some pimply faced schoolboy trying to get us off of this imaginary hook.
'Miss Tiffany Delamarre.' Judge Freeman glares down upon me, 'I have been informed that you have refused counsel, is this correct?'
'Yes your Honour.' I declare proudly.
'Foolish.' He booms, 'but admirable.'
As I am called to the stand I quickly squeeze Tracey's hand and whisper that everything will be okay.'
'Please state your name for the court.'

'Tiffany Delamarre.'

'Please raise your right hand.'

I do as I am told and can't help but momentarily feel like I am in a movie.

'Do you solemnly swear that the testimony you are about to give is the truth, the whole truth and nothing but the truth so help you God?'

I stifle a giggle and fight the urge to shout at the top of my lungs 'you can't handle the truth', but I feel my Jack Nicholson reference will not be taken lightly.

'I do.'

Judge Freeman shuffles a few loose papers and then looks directly at me, 'Miss Delamarre, please can you advise the court why you broke all of the regulations of Heaven and broke directly into Hell?'

Ooh straight into it then, fair enough. 'I was trying to save my friend.'

'From Hell? Surely you realise this is impossible.'

'No, not from Hell. My friend on Earth. You see I am investigating a beauty parlour that is using illegal substances in its products and the owner has disappeared. My friend Jodie was booked in for treatment and I had to stop her, but then I found that her boyfriend beats her up, so I had to stop that too.'

The Judge looks confused and who can blame him. 'Miss Delamarre what has any of that got to do with you breaking into Hell?'

'Well, I went undercover at the beauty parlour and found out that Juliana, my ex so called best friend is good friends with the owner, now here lies the problem. Juliana is in Hell for killing her little sister Maisie. So I had to get into Hell to speak to her and find out if she knew where I could find the owner of Pearl. Do you see?'

'Right. And did you find out the information that you required?'

'No. Lucifer has her locked up in some dingy little cell where all child killers go. She was deranged, but then I suppose you would be living in your own urine and faeces.'

'May I ask how you were able to return from Hell with such ease? It is my understanding that you are unable to use your wings.'

Are they mocking me? 'Lucifer walked me right to the front door.' I smile. I know that I shouldn't have said it, I know that I shouldn't make light of the situation, but how dare they laugh at my useless wings situation.

'You are on first name terms with this being?' He is not impressed.

'He could have kept me there, he could have refused to let me leave, but he did not. In fact he was perfectly civil to me throughout. I am not sorry that I went to Hell, I needed to. But I am sorry that I put so much faith into the people of Heaven. I would have thought that they would have stood by me, instead they throw me to the wolves.'

'Okay Miss Delamarre, there is no need for such dramatics. Please can you also explain to me your very clear insubordination towards this woman?' He points directly to Myra who by now has mastered such a look of sadness and distress that I almost pity her.

'She, your Honour, is a liar!'

Gasps echo around the court room as the Judge calls for order.

'Explain.'

'She is determined to take over Heaven, and she clearly

sees me as a threat!'

'And what makes you believe this?'

'Everything.'

'If you could elaborate on 'everything' that would be helpful.'

I fall silent. I know if I start ranting on about the changes she has made and how Celestia has changed they will just put it down to me being obstinate.

'I can't.'

'You can't elaborate?'

'No.'

'Very well, thank you for your information. You may now stand down. Miss Tracey Smith if you could please take the stand.'

I leave the stand, feeling Myra's eyes burning into me. I mouth an apology to Tracey and she just winks at me. I have no idea what she is going to say when she gets up there, but in all honesty it is unlikely to change the outcome. I blew it. 'Please state your name for the court.'

'Tracey Smith.'

'Please raise your right hand. Do you solemnly swear that the testimony you are about to give is the truth, the whole truth and nothing but the truth?'

'Yes.'

'Miss Tracey Smith please can you explain your role in aiding Miss Delamarre with her plan to infiltrate Hell?'

'I helped Tiffany because nobody else would.'

'Were you forced into this action by Miss Delamarre?'

'Nope. I did it because she is my best friend and friends stick together. I will tell you one thing though.' She pauses and points directly at Myra, 'If you believe anything that comes out of her mouth then you are an idiot. She is a liar and a deceiver. I hold my hands up to everything I did, and if you want to lock me in Limbo forever then I suggest you get on with it.'

'Miss Smith please...'

I watch in shock as Tracey leaves the stand and walks towards me, 'C'mon Tiff, I'd rather be in my cell than sit with these buffoons.'

Marching from the courtroom we hear Myra screeching that she told them so, that she was right, and then weirdly the Judge telling her to hush up.

'I'm sorry Tiff; I just couldn't stand there being questioned like we had done something wrong. Do you think I screwed up?'

'I don't think we had a leg to stand on from the second we were brought here.' I sigh.

Back in the cell I once again begin rattling the cell bars and demand that we are at least brought something to eat in this hellhole.

'No need Miss Delamarre. You are free to go.'

'Are you serious?'

Judge Freeman removes the cell key from his pocket and proceeds to release us. What on earth!

'Never in all of the years that I have been a Judge has anybody caused such disruption in my court room. I must say that I thoroughly enjoyed it. There will be no need for you to return for the verdict.'

'And what about Myra?' Questions Tracey angrily, 'she's the whole reason that we are in this mess.'

Myra will be dealt with by the courts; please do not fret about her for a moment longer. You are free to go ladies, you should be pleased.'

'That is it? No slap on the wrist? Community Service?

Nothing?' asks Tracey shocked.

'No. Though I will say that Celestia came through for you in the end, she must care for you more than you believed. Funny how things work out. I do have this for you though, from a Mr Daniel Fox.'

Taking the letter I am all at once filled with hope and relief, Daniel got us out just in the nick of time. Scanning the letter my eyes fill with tears.

'We have to go Judge Freeman, now!'

'What is it Tiff, what's happened?'

'It is Jodie. Dwight has attacked her. She's in the hospital.'

The room is white and sterile, just as hospitals should be I suppose, and there lay Jodie, her beautiful face black and blue and swollen.

Daniel met us outside of the building and brought us in. On the way I asked him how he had gotten us out of court, he said that he hadn't, that when he arrived back in Heaven Caleb told him what had happened and he went in search of Celestia but she was gone.

I suppose that was when she was having us released.

'Jodie.' I whisper, 'Can you hear me?'

She nods slowly, I ask her if she can remember what happened to her.

'There was a man.' She begins slowly, 'I've never seen him before, and he was just there, sitting in my armchair as if he owned it. I screamed and ran for the door, but he was fast, I didn't even see him move.' She begins crying and the doctor that has just entered suggests that we leave, we ignore him. 'I struggled but he was so strong. His arms were so strong around me, and that's how Dwight found us.'

'And what happened then?' I ask gently.

'Dwight went nuts, throwing things around the apartment, screaming and yelling. Not once did he try and get the stranger off of me, he was just frantic, saying over and over that he knew I was having an affair, that he'd finally caught me out. It's weird, but it was almost like he knew that the stranger was there, like he could see him, but not react to him. The next thing I knew I woke up here, Daniel found me when he was looking for you.'

'Did you see Dwight?' I ask Daniel.

'No, he was long gone.'

'Then it might not have been him that attacked me.'

Mutters Jodie.

'I'm sorry Jodie, but it was.' Begins Daniel, 'When I turned up you were laying in a heap on the floor whispering, 'I'm sorry Dwight, please don't hurt me Dwight', over and over.'

'Oh.' Her face crumples and she buries her head into the pillow and cries.

'Excuse me.' I turn to the doctor, 'is she, well you know.'

'Your friend has suffered a very vicious attack, the fact that she is awake and speaking is in my humble opinion a miracle. I do however think you should leave her to rest now.'

'Have the police been informed?' I ask, ignoring him again. 'She has refused to speak with them, and believe me we have tried.'

'Thank you doctor.'

Turning back to Jodie I promise her that Dwight won't ever come near her again, she mumbles something incoherent and pushes herself further into the pillow.

How could Dwight leave her to be attacked in her own home by a stranger and then attack her himself? How could Dwight not have been able to react to the stranger? Not see him?

Could the attacker have been Lucifer?

Just what is the Devil up to?

Chapter Fifteen

Two days after the appalling attack on Jodie she is finally home. She is subdued understandably, and wants to be left alone. I have told her that all she has to do is call through the wall if she needs anything. She just nodded and went into the bedroom.
I think that this assault is going to take a lot of healing from, and not just physically.
She still won't speak with the police, and I truly believe it is because she is half worried that Dwight will come back and finish what he started, and the other half is hopelessly still in love with him. I hope she comes to her senses soon.
Tracey has decided to take a day out from the investigation, to be honest she could take a week out we have that little to go on right now. She needs to spend some time with Caleb and reconnect with him.
Daniel got called back to his case unexpectedly, so the things we had planned for today have been scrapped.
Instead I intend to have a lazy day lounging around in my pyjamas and reading trashy magazines. First however is a long, hot bubble bath.
Easing myself into the sweet smelling hot water I close my eyes and let my mind drift far away, such bliss, such decadence.
'Beautiful.'
Screaming I grab the towel and drag into the bath, what the hell!
'You do not need to be shy around me.' Lucifer grins, 'I enjoy to see such perfection laid out before me. Like a

wonderful banquet.'

'Get out of here right now you perv!' I yell.

'There is no need to yell, and may I advise you that screaming is also another avenue not worth taking. Your neighbours are out and Jodie is so drugged that I doubt she would hear an aeroplane landing in her front room.'

'Whatever! Get out!'

'I cannot, we have a lot to discuss, and this setting is perfect.'

'What do you want from me Lucifer? I have told you numerous times that I have no interest in you whatsoever and yet still you pursue me. Do not think for even a second that I don't know that it was you that broke into Jodie's apartment and attacked her!'

'Attack? I merely stopped her from making a scene.'

'You are such a bad liar! You knew that Dwight was on his way didn't you? You knew exactly what he would do to her. Are you having my friends beaten to a pulp now so that I'll agree to go with you and then you'll stop? I don't have many friends, so you might want to think of a new strategy.'

'You wound me with your accusations young Tiffany. If I wanted to hurt you I would pay a little visit to your parents, maybe pop around for tea. Do you think they would be more welcoming of me?'

'Stay away from them or so help me god.'

'What will you do? I am intrigued to know.'

'I will never be yours Lucifer, never.' I spit.

'Then we have a problem. I want you Tiffany Delamarre, and I will have you.'

'What is it going to take for you to understand? I do not belong with you, I have no business being in Hell, I don't want you.'

'But you dream of me, do you not?'

I do not even know why I am shocked, of course my weird nightmare was down to him, why else would my brain put me through so much pain.

'I should have known.' I sigh, 'you know, if you wanted to paint yourself in a much better light then maybe in that heinous nightmare you shouldn't have locked me in stinking cage and then left me to be mauled.'

'I would never let that happen to you, join me and you will see firsthand what a gentleman I can be.'

'I would rather gouge out my own eyeballs, eat glass and vomit piranhas than join you in anything. Can you not just take a hint? There are a gazillion demented women in the world that would no doubt love to be your plaything, go and find one of them!'

'They are not you, so therefore they are inadequate.'

'I am going to say this to you just one more time, I.Do.Not.Want.Anything.To.Do.With.You.Physcho!'

'I see.' He stands and turns his back to me. 'Then you leave me no choice.'

'Leave you no choice about what?'

'I shall have to work even harder to impress you. Be warned however that I make no apologies for the people that are harmed along the way. Good day Tiffany.'

I yell for him to come back and explain himself. Nothing. What am I going to do with this brain dead idiot?

Why does he not understand that I do not want him? And what could he have up his sleeve that could possibly impress me? Nothing good I imagine. I have a feeling that what impresses him would disgust most people.

Great! I have just made a monster out of the Devil.

Chapter Sixteen

A week after the attack and my rather interesting bath, Jodie has suggested that we go wedding dress shopping. I have to say that I was surprised. She seems to have bounced back to her old self and assured me that A) she is fine, and B) she will be speaking to the police. I told her that I will go with her if she needs me, but she said that she feels it is something that she needs to do alone, to feel stronger.

I can't pretend to understand what she is going through, she thought that Dwight was perfect and then he destroyed the illusion with his fists and cruel words. I do know though that she is strong and she deserves so much better than that pleb.

So here we are, picking up the pieces, Jodie from her tattered love life, Tracey from a million dreadful things in her past that I know she will never fully divulge, and me from a failed life, failed case and the worst person you could ever have stalking you.

Standing outside of the most exclusive bridal boutique that we could find I am incredibly nervous. I cannot quite believe that I am here, engaged and ready to try on bridal gowns. Insane.

Everything in the window display seems to sparkle and dazzle me, like diamond heaven. Tiaras, long satin gloves, glitzy jewellery, shoes!

Pulling the girls through the big glass doors a twinkly bell above announces our arrival.

'Ooooh who's the lucky girl then?' Coos the way over tanned, way too skinny and definitely way too giddy sales assistant. 'Lucky, lucky, lucky.' She chants repeatedly whilst eyeballing us. Okaaay!

With a mighty shove Tracey pushes me towards the crazy lady and declares loudly that I am the lucky, lucky, lucky girl. I groan inwardly and smile.

Within fifteen minutes of being in the boutique the girls have been seated, champagne has been handed around to everyone and I have been stripped down to my bra and pants.

I find myself sort of hovering around semi naked in the changing rooms wishing a great big hole would swallow me up. No such luck.

I can hear Tracey and Jodie discussing my wedding in graphic detail, whilst paying absolutely zero attention to their freezing cold, distressed friend.

The shop assistant has already reprimanded me for not wearing my actual bridal lingerie, and while I stood there shivering she explained that it is much easier to find a gown if they have an idea of my bridal lingerie.

My response to this bizarre and rather unreasonable demand was as follows;

'Oh, I did not realise, after all I have never done this before. However if you would be kind enough to direct me to the nearest Ann Summers I would be delighted to repurchase my crotch less panties and peephole bra just for you.'

Hearing the rising anger in my voice Tracey and Jodie rush to the changing rooms to calm down the situation. At last!

I have been handed five dresses that I would not be seen

dead in, which is funny considering that I am dead. I have refused them all and she is not pleased.

'Now then.' Trills the hyper assistant, 'This should suit you splendidly.'

The dress is a toilet roll cover! A big poufy meringue toilet roll cover, no chance!

Why is she so obsessed with the big dresses!

'No. Look I need you to listen to me, no more interfering, no more giddy suggestions. I know what I want, and what I want is that dress over there.'

She looks at me as though I have just told her that she's adopted. 'But...'

'No buts, I want that one!'

'But that is a Vera Wang exclusive.'

'And?' I ask impatiently.

'And it's fifteen thousand pounds.'

'Please just bring me the dress.'

With a grunt and mumbling something about my being Bridezilla she stomps off and brings me the dress that I requested.

Stepping into the gown Tracey pulls it up over my body and holds it in place whilst Jodie buttons me up. The dress is white silk with little pearl buttons running all the way down the back. It fits snugly to my chest and then flairs out slightly from the waist. It has a small train which is just perfect. It is not strapless as I had envisaged I would choose, but instead has thin little straps that look like plaits.

'You look stunning.' Sighs Jodie, wiping a tear from her eye.

Tracey seems lost for words, but she gives me a big hug and nods her approval.

'This is the one.' I declare happily. 'I would like to order this one.'

The shop assistant smiles, no doubt mentally totalling up her commission and places my order quickly. No doubt so I cannot change my mind.

'And shoes?' she asks.

I smile. 'Do you sell Louboutins?'

Her look of confusion tells me everything.

'No then, no shoes. Now, if you could please sort out my friends here with their bridesmaid dresses that would be marvellous.'

Squeals ring out through the boutique as Tracey and Jodie throw themselves upon me.

'Oh my god! Bridesmaids!' They both squeak. 'What will we choose, there are so many.'

'May I ask what your intended colour scheme is?'

I look at the shop assistant and realise that I have no idea. With everything that has been going on lately I haven't had the chance to just stop and think about the wedding, even when I do get a spare moment alone the Devil stalks me.

Not that she would understand any of that. What would Daniel like? Do guys even care about the colour of things?

'Tiff?' Jodie waves her hand in front of my face, 'Earth to Tiffany, you in there?'

'I don't know.' I murmur.

'What, you don't know if you're in there?' laughs Tracey hysterically.

'I don't know what colour.' I know that I sound dopey and confused, but I am.

'How about we start with your favourite colour?' suggests the sales assistant.

'Pink. But is pink too much? Would Daniel approve of pink?'

'Honey, Daniel won't care if we turn up in black bags, he will only have eyes for you, and in that dress so will all the other blokes.'

The shop assistant ushers Tracey and Jodie into the changing rooms with a heap of dresses and I am handed even more champagne. They are giggling like little girls and I have to laugh out loud when Tracey announces that she has holes in her socks.

What would I do without these two?

How could I have flitted through my life thinking that I had friends, when truthfully I had no idea what the word friendship even meant.

All of the people that I have encountered since dying have all at one point or another taught me something important. I wish that I could go back and see everybody one last time, show them how I have grown, how I have changed.

Would my parents be proud of the change in me?

Would they even take time out of their pompous lives to care?

I guess I will never know.

Flinging back the curtain Tracey and Jodie make a rather dramatic entrance in the most hideous pink ensemble that I have ever seen, there is no way they are being seen out in public dressed like that! Tiffany to the rescue again.

It is going to be a long day.

Chapter Seventeen

'Hey sleepyhead, wake up, you've got mail.' Tracey bounces on my bed and then squirms and wriggles until she is underneath the duvet with me. 'Did you hear me? Mail!'

'Soooo?' I groan, 'it's just mail, I have had it before you know, it's not exactly a new thing.'

'Yeah I know that dopey, but nobody knows you're here! As far as the world is concerned you are busy being eaten by worms and christ knows what other creepy crawlies... soooo mail is a pretty big deal.'

Pushing back the covers I reach for the envelope that Tracey is busy wafting in front of my face and quickly scan the front. No stamp or address, just my name scrawled in some old fashioned calligraphy.

Tiffany Delamarre.

Ripping open the seal it only takes me a few moments to read the contents.

Alicia King, Room 25 of the Durkar Roods Hotel, Meltham. Be quick.

Who would give me the whereabouts of Alicia King?

I can only think of one person, and if I am correct then that can only mean one thing.

Lucifer's twisted games have just begun.

Pulling up outside of the hotel in our recently 'acquired' car, don't ask, Tracey's past strikes again. We rush into the reception area and ring the little bell on the front desk.

'We should just go up there.' I whisper impatiently.

'Clearly nobody is coming.'

Nodding her agreement we make a dash for the stairs to the right of us.

'Can I help you?' A snooty voice follows our movements and we halt, could we look anymore suspicious?

'Nah, we're all good ta.' Trills Tracey, 'cheers anyway.'

'I'm sorry, but could you just wait a moment, are you guests here?'

'Well no, not exactly...' I begin.'

'In that case can you explain why you are going up the stairs so hastily?'

'We know somebody staying here, so if you don't mind.' I finish in a snooty voice of my own.

'And who would that be?'The woman asks with a disbelieving smirk.

Not wanting to cause a scene in front of the new arrivals in the reception area, I point them out to little miss snobby pants and whilst she is busy saying welcome to them we make a run for it.

'Bloody hell, she was determined not to let us go anywhere.' Pants Tracey, 'Security here is tighter than MI5.'

Room 25 looms before us and I admit to Tracey that I am petrified at what we will find.

Voices from down the staircase alert us instantly to the fact that security has been called, we have no choice now but to go in, being caught is not an option.

Slowly turning the doorknob I listen carefully for any sign of life. It is completely silent in there.

'Get in already, they're coming.' Squeals Tracey, shoving me through the door. 'You'd make a useless copper, way too slow!'

The smell that hits us is overpowering, but I recognise it. Where from though?

The room is in complete darkness so I make my away across to the windows and fling open the curtain.

'Oh god tiff, I'm gonna puke.' Mutters Tracey.

Turning slowly, I take a steadying breath. I gasp as I take in the scene before me. What has he done? Oh god, what has he done?

The body of Alicia King lays spread-eagled on the huge four poster bed, empty Formaldehyde bottles are littered everywhere and I now know why the smell is so familiar to me.

Her naked body is covered from head to toe in nasty looking blisters, some weeping, others looking as though they would pop with even the slightest touch.

Her eyes are open and blood shot, and her mouth is open, forever in a permanent scream.

'Who would do this Tiff? It's sick?'

I gag as I look over her once more, 'I know exactly who would do this, I also know that he won't stop until I'm his.'

'What? Look Tiff we can figure this out later, but right now we need to get out of here!'

'There is no way out, the lobby will be swarming with security and management trying to find us.'

'We need a diversion.' I look around the room for any kind of inspiration, my eyes automatically refusing to see the deformed body on the bed. 'Okay how about...'

The wailing siren drowns out my voice as I acknowledge that Tracey has set off the fire alarm.

'Looks like we got ourselves an inferno.' She laughs, 'Run!'

The reception area is a hive of manic delirium, and we manage to slip through unnoticed. It's amazing how people put so much faith in a noise. They have no evidence of a fire, they cannot smell burning and yet like little sheep they follow the most hysterical person that they can find, convinced that they know best. All common sense disappears.

In the safety of the car we both let out nervous laughs and wonder what to do next.
'Tiff is there something that you want to tell me about all of that up there?'
'What do you mean?' I ask, even though I know perfectly well what she means.
'You said, and I quote: I know exactly who did this; I also know that he won't stop until I'm his. What did you mean?'
'It's Lucifer, he's stalking me.' I cry. 'I told him to get lost and he promised that he would up his game to get me. I do not know what to do. Is all of that in the bedroom my fault?'
'Don't be retarded.' She slaps my arm, 'It's not your fault the Devil is a nutjob!'
'He won't stop though, not until I agree to be his, and I do not under any circumstances want to be his! But how many more people will he kill to try and get me?'
'You are stronger than this Tiffany snooty knickers Delamarre, so stop whining, wipe ya face and pull ya socks up. Got it?!'
'I'm not wearing any socks.' I sniffle.
'Dumbass! C'mon let's get out of here before they notice two strange girls loitering in the car park and a random

stinking corpse in the bedroom.'

'I suppose we don't need to finish the case now with Alicia dead.'

'Yeah, sort of anticlimactic thought don't you think.'

'Mmm I guess. I don't know what I was hoping for in this case, but it certainly wasn't this'

'Well it's done. Shall I put some tunes on?'

I nod, wipe my eyes and lean back into the seat. My mind empty, at least for a little while.

...In other news, Police are today investigating a fire that has broken out at a beauty spa in Leeds. Pearl Beauty Spa and Detox Centre has been at the centre of a city wide controversy over the past few months, with alleged clients making serious allegations about the company. The owner, a Miss Alicia King has yet to be located. West Yorkshire Police are urging any witnesses to contact them directly...

'Oh.My.God!' gasps Tracey, shocked.

'Kimberley!' I shout, 'She would have been working today, we need to get there now.'

'Calm down Tiff, think rationally. We can't just rock up and ask if anybody has burnt to death in the building can we.'

'I can say that I worked there, that I am a concerned colleague.'

'You are dead! Dead girls do not work in beauty spa's.'

'But I need to know!' I hit the dashboard in anger and feel Tracey's eyes burning into me.

'Then we will go to Heaven and see if she is being processed, but we are not under any circumstances going to that crime scene – got it?!'

Forty minutes later we pull up outside of a still smouldering Pearl and I rush out of the car towards the door. Tracey did in all respect try her hardest to dissuade me, but she is clearly no match for my powers of persuasion.

'Excuse me miss, but you need to come away from there.' The police officer moves me away from the doorway and sits me down at the curb side, my distress clearly visible.

'Do you know if anybody was inside?' I croak.

'I'm afraid that I can't release that information miss. Are you a family member of the...' He stops, knowing full well that he has just given me my answer.

She was inside.

Lucifer set fire to the building while Kimberley was still inside.

Two murders in one day, and at least one of them was totally innocent of any wrongdoings in her young life. He just left her to burn alive!

Shaking my head I make my way back towards the car. If he thinks for even a moment that he can kill innocent people and I will be impressed then he needs a serious reality check.

I will not be his... I will not.

Chapter Eighteen

It's been four days since the hotel incident; Tracey has also confirmed with the processing team that Kimberley Payne was indeed killed in the arson attack on Pearl.

I am avoiding Heaven at the moment, I have no interest in going back there until Celestia apologises for betraying me. In all fairness I do not even know what I would say to her. I do not know how we can get past this.

There was a moment after my death that Celestia was wonderful, not immediately of course because I know she despised me. But that day in the cemetery where she stood by me and comforted me was something that I will always remember, and now she has ruined it.

I know that I am not always her favourite person, I am opinionated, shallow at times and most definitely vocal, but I believed deep down that we had moved on from that. I know that I have not totally changed my ways, but I do know that I am a better person than the one that showed up in Heaven and disrupted the queue like a mad woman. I just do not understand how she could have stabbed me in the back like that.

Daniel has been wonderful throughout this case, despite the fact that I have rarely seen him, due to his commitments with his undercover case, the moments that we have managed to snatch have been wonderful.

He told me that he is proud of me for the way I have handled the Jodie / Dwight situation, though I beg to differ on that one. I was too blunt, too forceful, as is the norm with me. I know that I should have just let Jodie take her time and come to the realisation herself that Dwight was no good for her. But my fear was that she did not have the luxury of time. He would have continued to beat on her and make her feel worthless. How could I let my new friend suffer in such a way?

I had a little moment today with Daniel where I had the sudden realisation that my father would not be able to walk me down the aisle when Daniel and I are married. I know that it shouldn't upset me, my father was never really there for me during my life, throwing his gold card at me and paying me a rather generous allowance every month was as close to being a father as he ever got. But still, the tradition of my father giving me away at my wedding will never be upheld. It saddens me.

I have no thoughts about my mother; I mean the woman turned my wake into a social event for crying out loud. I doubt that she would have been fully there with me, choosing a gown, trying on silly hats, making wedding plans late into the night.

The fact of the matter is that I am alone now, an orphan. The only people that have stood by me, and at times when I did not deserve it are the people that I hurt. Funny how things work out.

I only have one thing left to sort out now, and if this does not work then I am at a loss of what to do.

My graveside is cold and deserted. What is it with these places, always so grim?

Pulling my hood closer around my face I yell for him at the top of voice.

'LUCIFER! YOU GET DOWN HERE RIGHT THIS INSTANT!'

I feel stupid of course. Should anybody turn up and hear me I plan to tell them that Lucifer is my cat and he is stuck in the big oak tree that shadows my headstone.

'LUCIFER!'

'Why all of the shouting? You merely needed to whisper and I would have come to you.'

'Listen moron, this has to stop okay! You and I? Never going to happen.'

'Oh Tiffany, how my heart slowly breaks at this news, why do you not understand that I will never cease chasing you?'

'Why do you not understand that I will never cease hating you?'

'Did you like my gift to you?' he smirks.

'Two dead bodies? Not really my kind of thing.'

'I helped you though, did I not? I feel it only fair that you repay the favour.'

'I never asked you to kill anybody for me! I never asked you to set fire to that building and burn Kimberley alive!'

'Collateral damage, I could see no way around it.'

'Can you hear yourself? You burnt a young woman to death! You covered another woman in Formaldehyde and let her skin blister and burn! At what point during any of that did you figure that I would be impressed? Did you honestly believe that I would throw myself at you?'

'Of course not.' He laughs, 'I know that you are bad Tiffany, not sick. I was making a point, and I do believe that my point hit the mark. I told you what I would do to get you, can you see now just what I am prepared to do?'

'It is never going to happen!'

'I have an eternity of destruction that I can bring your way Tiffany. Why would you choose that over being with me?'

'Because I hate you, I despise everything about you! I would prefer to spend all of eternity and beyond locked in one of your nasty little cages then ever be with you!'

'That can be arranged.'

'Dream on loser! I do not belong with you, I belong in Heaven.'

'Juliana misses you. In fact she screams your name over and over in her sleep, why is that do you think?'

His curveball throws me. 'I don't know, maybe because you make her dream of me?'

'No, no. She dreams of you because you put her where she is.'

'I had nothing to do with the reasons that she was sent to Hell and you know that. She killed her little sister!'

'But you could have stopped her from being murdered, and she thinks about that every day.'

'I tried to stop it, she wouldn't listen!'

'Maybe you didn't try hard enough.'

'Why do you even care?'

'Oh I don't, but you do. Not to worry though, when you are finally mine we will remove all of these silly notions and ideas from your brain. Can't have a partner that is sentimental now, can I.'

'Partner! Don't make me laugh.'

'You will come to me Tiffany; for the repercussions of your constant rebuffs are not something that I feel you are prepared to deal with.'

'I am begging you; please do not hurt anybody else. Just understand that you and I will never be together, please.'

'Begging does not suit you; you know what you have to do.'

'Please?' I ask one more time, weary, defeated.

'Oh, one more thing. Your parents are doing very well... without you.'

Throwing myself to the ground I bury my head in my hands and cry. How could he do this?

Chapter Nineteen

Flipping off the living room lights I make my way blind into my bedroom and feel for my pyjamas. I am used to the layout of the apartment now and will be sorry to give it up. I find the darkness in here soothing, it's like when I have turned out the lights in my apartment I have also turned out the lights in my mind. Everything becomes peaceful, normal. I feel normal.

Its only 8pm but my bed is calling. Daniel is still undercover, Tracey is visiting Caleb and Jodie just fancied a night in reading. I have no other plans for my evening, so I figure catching up on some sleep is a good idea.

Slipping under the cotton sheets I close my eyes and let the day wash away from me. I can feel sleep reaching out to me, its arms warm and welcoming, beckoning me.

I want to go, but I cannot. Something feels wrong, off kilter.

Dread runs down my body as I realise that I am no longer alone in my bedroom.

Icy cold fear snakes down my spine and my heartbeat trebles in speed. I know that it isn't Lucifer, not so soon after our last encounter, and he would not be so deviant as to creep up on me in the dark, he is much too forward for that.

I dare not breathe as footsteps near my bed, the weight of the intruder making the floorboards creak. The dark no longer seems so soothing.

'I know you're awake, I can smell your fear.' The voice murmurs softly.

I whimper, I cannot help it. 'Who are you?'

'You mean you don't recognise my voice? I thought all you street whores were good at detecting things in the dark?'

'Dwight?'

'The one and only. I think you and I have some unfinished business, shame that friend of yours isn't here to join in.' I hear the clink of metal, 'As I recall handcuffs are a particular favourite of yours.'

'Please don't do this... I'm begging you.'

'Ah begging, just up my street.' I feel him lean over the bed, his breath hot in my ear, 'I'm gonna make you beg like the dirty little...'

The bedroom light snaps on and I am momentarily blinded. I can hear Daniel's voice, angry. Scrambling from the bed I trip on the sheets tangled around my ankles and fall forwards. As my head connects with the bedside cabinet I feel blood dripping down my face. Great!

Kicking free of the sheets I rush into the living room, Daniel has Dwight pinned to the floor and he is reigning punches onto his already bloodied face.

Dwight wriggles and somehow he has now become the attacker. He has Daniel trapped between the breakfast bar and his solid body.

Looking around I grab the nearest thing to me, the meat cleaver from the butchers block. So help me god the second that I do this I will be dragged kicking and screaming straight into Lucifer's arms. Raising the cleaver I say a quick prayer and bring it down.

'Nooooo!' Jodie's scream echoes around the tiny room. As she tackles me to the ground I drop the cleaver, winded.

'Get off of me you idiot.' I yell at Jodie.

Scrambling to my feet I push Jodie out of the way and hit Dwight over the head with the entire butchers block. He stops moving instantly.

'You've killed him!' Cries out Jodie, rushing to his side, 'You've bloody killed him!'

'Yes well, good riddance.' I declare.

'Are you hurt honey?' asks Daniel worriedly, 'Let me look at you.'

'I'm fine.'

'Fine? You have blood running down your face! I'll kill him!'

'Stop, seriously! I bumped my head getting out of bed to save you.'

'To save me?' he howls in laughter, 'To save me?'

'Shut up Daniel.' I snap.

'You've killed him.' Jodie's voice, so small draws our attention to the scene in front of us.

'Is he really dead?' I ask Daniel, scared.

He reaches down and checks Dwight's pulse, a frown appearing on his handsome face.

'Unfortunately... no!'

'Oh thank god, thank god.' Jodie is nearing hysteria and I feel I may have to slap her face to bring her out of it. How can she be happy that this twit is still alive and kicking?

'Can you wake him up?' She pleads with Daniel, 'I need to talk to him.'

Oh great!

Daniel slaps Dwight's face a few times until he begins to stir.

'What the hell...' he groans, 'where am I?'

'You are lucky to be alive is what you are.' Begins Jodie.

'Jodie? Baby?'

'Now you listen real close to me...'

'Jodie... I...'

'Shut up! I do not love you; in fact I don't even like you. You are a coward and I want you out of my life for good, do you understand?'

Dwight looks as though he has just had his favourite toy taken away. Jodie however has never looked so strong, so empowered.

'If I so much as see your face, hear your voice or smell your cheap disgusting aftershave anywhere near me or my friends again I swear to god I will kill you myself! How dare you ever think it's acceptable to raise your hand to a woman? You are nothing but a low life scumbag, now get out!'

He does not move, just lays there shocked, unsure. 'NOW!' she screams.

Scrambling to his feet he shuffles his way out of my apartment and out of Jodie's life for good. His tail firmly tucked between his legs.

Taking Jodie's hand I lead her to the settee and go to put the kettle on.

'Do you have anything stronger?' she asks wearily.

'You're damn straight she has – Sambuca baby! I cannot believe that I have missed the Dwight showdown! Bloody hell girls, heads up next time!' Tracey, larger than life as always pours the shots and passes them around, 'let's partaaaaay ladies!'

'Erm, where's Daniel?' I wonder out loud.

'Outside.' Answers Tracey, 'making sure that clown doesn't return, soooo, let's get drunk and dance like loons!'

Shutting the door, I raise my shot glass high in the air and

make a toast:
'To good friends, never shall a man come between a lady and her ladies. Cheers!'

Chapter Twenty

Sitting once again in Celestia's office I take a deep breath and wait for her to speak. I decided to bite the bullet and make the first move. At the end of the day she owes me an apology and I do not feel we can move on from any of this until I have received it.

'Tiffany.' She begins timidly, 'I did you wrong and I would like to extend my deepest regrets for the way that I treated you. I cannot for the life of me explain why I took the action that I did towards you and Tracey, I wish that she were here so that I could apologise to her too. Is she avoiding me?'

I laugh, 'Not at all, Tracey doesn't hold grudges, and as far as she's concerned it is all water under the bridge.'

'And you? Do you hold a grudge against me?'

'I did.' I admit truthfully. 'You betrayed me Celestia. I have worked so hard on this case and yet your trust in me was so easy to shatter. Myra came along with her strong ideas and notions of a better Heaven and you cast me aside just to please her. I am just thankful that you came to your senses when you did.'

'I am truly sorry for what I have done. Can you ever forgive me?'

I pause dramatically, more for effect than anything else. 'I already have.' I smile, 'But please, in future can you just have a little faith in me?'

'Yes. Yes I can.'

'Great! Well, you'll be pleased to know that Jodie has moved on from Dwight, a relief for her mother as well I should imagine. She has moved apartments just in case Dwight ever does decide to find her again, and she has given up on the idea of any kind of beauty treatment, though to be honest that was all Dwight's idea as well. I wish that I could have saved Alicia and Kimberley, but with Lucifer against me I had no chance.'

'Yes, Daniel has explained the situation with Lucifer. Do you feel that you need some time out from your cases? A bodyguard maybe?'

'No. Lucifer has no intention of hurting me, in his sick twisted little mind he thinks that if he causes enough destruction to the people that I care about I will run to him and it will stop.'

'Do you think that he will ever stop chasing you?'

'Eventually he will, he won't have any choice in the matter.'

'How so?'

'There is nobody left on earth that I love or care for deeply enough that it would make me choose him. My life before was a lie.'

'And your parents? If he targets them?'

'That is a bridge that I will have to cross should it ever arise. Right now I just want to celebrate my engagement to Daniel properly and be thankful that nobody else was hurt during this case. If you are putting me on another case could I please request one that is a little less stressful and full on?'

'I wish I could.' She sighs, 'but those cases are very rare, and anyway, I thought you enjoyed a challenge?'

'Could I at least have one that has less dead people in it then?'

'A strange comment to make for a person surrounded by

dead people.'

'You know what I mean. Seriously Celestia, I don't think I can handle anymore corpses.'

Handing me a very thick manila envelope she smiles. The front cover reads TOP SECRET and I just know from the weight of this file that I am in for another bugger of a case. 'I know that you will do your best.' She winks.

Flipping open the cover the words 'speed dating', 'commune' and 'mental illness' spring out at me. Great! 'Leave it for now. Go out and celebrate with your friends, okay.'

'Would you like to come?' I ask, unsure of what her response will be.

'I would love to.' She beams, 'I thought you would never ask.'

Bar Salsa is once again heaving, but we manage to find a spot right next to the karaoke machine and the bar, perfect. Jodie looks amazing tonight; I suppose this is what happens when you finally free yourself from the shackles that have been weighing you down for so long.

Daniel is at the bar with Caleb, and Victoria and Celestia are deep in conversation at the table. The night could not be more perfect.

I am surrounded by everybody that I love in the world (minus the kids, Maisie and Sophie) and my shock surprise for the evening? Damien has turned up. I have no idea who invited him, but I am glad that they did. He has been such a massive help during the last two cases, and even though we didn't get off to the best of starts, he has become one of the gang.

Taking to the microphone Jodie shocks us all by

announcing that she would like to say a few words. The bar quietens down as she begins to speak.

'A few weeks ago I met the most amazing girls. These girls have now become the best of friends to me. I had some issues that needed dealing with, and in true best friend style they came, they saw and they conquered. Thanks to them I am now the free woman that you see standing before you, and I just wanted to say thanks.' The entire bar erupts into cheers and woops as music begins to play on the karaoke machine. 'I would like to dedicate this song to my two new friends, who could come up here and help me if they wanted? Please.' She laughs nervously as the music really starts to kick in now.

Making our way across to the Karaoke machine and our awaiting microphones we sing with all of our might. The perfect choice for the perfect ending.

You don't own me

I'm not just one of your many toys

You don't own me

Don't say I can't go with other boys

Babababababaaaaaaaaaaaaaaaaaaaaa

Don't tell me what to do

And don't tell me what to say

And when I go out with you

Don't put me on display

You don't own me

Don't try to change me in any way

You don't own me

Don't drag me down

'Cause I'll never stay

I don't tell you what to say

I don't tell you what to do

So just let me be myself

That's all I ask of you

I'm young

And I love to be young

I'm free

And I love to be free

To live my life the way that I want

To say and do whatever I please

You don't own me

Printed in Poland
by Amazon Fulfillment
Poland Sp. z o.o., Wrocław